FINDING ELIZABETH

DEBRA MELLER

Copyright © 2020 Debra Meller

The right of Debra Meller to be identified as the Author of the Work has been asserted by her in accordance to the Copyright, Designs and Patents Act 1988.

First published in 2020 by Bloodhound Books

Apart from any use permitted under UK copyright law, this publication may only be reproduced, stored, or transmitted, in any form, or by any means, with prior permission in writing of the publisher or, in the case of reprographic production, in accordance with the terms of licences issued by the Copyright Licensing Agency.

All characters in this publication are fictitious and any resemblance to real persons, living or dead, is purely coincidental.

www.bloodhoundbooks.com

Print ISBN 978-1-913942-03-8

ALSO BY DEBRA MELLER

The Asylum

Dedicated to my son, Brian, who will always be forever young.

PROLOGUE

As the year 1912 was approaching, Elizabeth was becoming increasingly unsettled and her diary, that was discovered years later, told a story of a young woman that longed for the notoriety she believed she deserved.

On 8 December, she wrote, *How sad are those that settle for a life unfulfilled. A life of servitude, and one that often ends without ever being recognised for something extraordinary. I will never be held down by another, I will always remain independent, my art will become my reality, my life's work, and if I tire of this, I will simply move on to my next adventure. When I am dead and gone, my name and my accomplishments will live on and I will never be forgotten, of this I am certain.*

The house at the end of Carlton Lane in the town of Briarwood was much like the others in this affluent area. A two-storey, four-bedroom home with a lovely rose garden that swept along the path to the front door. It had been in the Hamilton family for generations and had been left to Eric Hamilton when his mother passed away in 1908.

Eric had done well over the years, and was the owner of a successful garment factory in the East Riding of Yorkshire. He had married late in life and from the very beginning his wife Kathleen proved to be a handful. She had a wicked temper that would only escalate when she didn't get what she wanted. On at least one occasion a constable was called in to calm her down. By all accounts, the Hamiltons had a very tumultuous marriage, yet Eric did nothing to improve this situation.

By December of 1911, Kathleen had moved her mother Edna and younger sister Leah into their home, escalating the conflict. As if this wasn't enough, she later insisted her grandmother Ivy join them. Eric initially tried to stop the influx of Kathleen's relatives, but failed miserably. Whenever she didn't get what she wanted, she threatened to spread vicious rumours about his extramarital affairs.

By March of 1912, the Hamilton household had reached full capacity, but Kathleen didn't stop there. A few weeks after Ivy moved in, she hired a live-in maid, without her husband's knowledge or approval. By now every room in their home was occupied, except the space Eric used as his study. This didn't matter to Kathleen and as her husband stood idly by, his wife emptied this room, moving all his belongings into the attic. This cramped, dusty space was now the only place left in his home where he could call his own and where he could avoid Kathleen and the rest of her obnoxious family.

By late April, the neighbours noticed that they hadn't seen or heard Kathleen in days. This was very unusual, but most thought that Eric had finally come to his senses and sent his wife and her family packing. Everyone knew that they had been sponging off Eric for some time and no one would have blamed him if this was exactly what he did.

Although the Hamilton household did seem eerily quiet, Eric's neighbours weren't complaining, as they were now enjoying the peace that had finally returned to Carlton Lane.

1

Eric Hamilton was not in the habit of staying away from his garment factory for more than a few days at a time. Mr Hamilton had not been in to work for six days straight. His foreman, Robert Carlyle was becoming concerned. Although Mr Hamilton had complained of feeling poorly on the morning prior to his absence, no one expected him to be away this long.

Carlyle had been with the company for almost eighteen years and when Mr Hamilton wasn't there, he was in charge. He was responsible for overseeing the entire factory and making sure that the garments leaving the factory were of the highest quality. Everything had run smoothly – until the day the employees were expecting their pay packet.

As the workers entered the factory on that May morning in 1912, Mr Hamilton wasn't there to greet them.

Robert tried to reassure the workers that this was simply an oversight, but as the day wore on with no sign of Mr Hamilton, the sixty-three men and forty-four women employed at the factory became increasingly agitated. They relied entirely on the money they earned.

Robert was also somewhat confused; he had never known

his boss to neglect his employees or his responsibilities. He had already missed one meeting with a client and if he didn't come in to work the following day, he would miss another.

Robert also had a large family to feed and although he had saved a few shillings, it wouldn't last. He had tried to call Mr Hamilton several times by telephone that morning and didn't receive an answer.

By 4pm, the workers were becoming more and more agitated by the delay and Robert had no choice but to confront this problem head-on. 'I'll get to the bottom of this,' he told the crowd of anxious workers. 'I'll go to Briarwood tomorrow morning as soon as I've opened the factory doors. There'll be a simple explanation for it, that I can promise. I'll return with your pay packets by day's end.'

Early the following morning, Robert stood outside the factory doors and after the last employee had taken their place, still wearing his heavy apron and factory attire, he cycled over to Carlton Lane. Neighbours that were outside enjoying the lovely warm weather stared at him as he rode down Carlton Lane. It was warmer than usual and the sunshine was a welcome relief after several weeks of continuous rain and cold temperatures.

Robert was nervous as he walked up the path that led to the Hamilton's house. He had never been to Mr Hamilton's home and he felt that somehow he was overstepping his authority. Still, he knew that the employees were anxious for their pay packets and he couldn't return empty-handed.

As he stood looking up at the house, everything appeared normal on the outside. The rose bushes that were already in bloom had been deadheaded and the grass had been cut recently. The curtains in the parlour were drawn and the only noise he could hear was from the horses in the coach house. The neighbour across the street watched his every move from her front garden.

A few seconds later, after taking a deep breath, he knocked on the heavy wooden door. Robert listened, but he didn't hear any movement inside. He knocked again, this time with a little more force, but still no response.

Robert hadn't travelled this far to go back without answers, so he bravely opened the letterbox and shouted in. It was then that he noticed a putrid smell so overpowering he had to back away from the door. As he stood on the porch wondering what on earth that smell was, he saw the gardener trimming some trees on the opposite side of the Hamilton's property. He shouted to the man but the distance was too great.

Robert then walked to the back gate, still watched by the woman across the road.

One of the Hamilton's horses was desperately trying to reach a bale of hay that was a few feet from where he had been tied. Robert released the horse allowing him to eat freely then called out to the gardener again. This time he turned around and waved.

After explaining who he was and why he was there, Robert led Jessie the gardener around the back of the house to see if they could see anything unusual.

Jessie told Robert that he had worked for the Hamilton family for almost twenty years and although he didn't know Eric Hamilton well, he had known his mother and father. After checking every window, neither of them could find a way in or see anything unusual inside. Most of the windows had heavy curtains on them and the smaller ones were too high to give a good view inside.

Then Robert took Jessie around to the front of the house. 'What do you think of that smell?' he asked the gardener.

Jessie opened the mail slot and like Robert, he slowly backed away. 'I think it's time to summon a constable.' Jessie had smelled the same putrid smell before and he knew exactly what it was.

Robert, on the other hand, wasn't so sure, but he did as Jessie asked. Not long after, he returned with a constable from the Briarwood Police Station.

By now the O'Donnell family from across the street and some other neighbours were standing on the Hamilton's porch.

The constable spoke to Robert and Jessie briefly than banged on the Hamilton's door with such force that the beautiful stained-glass window cracked. When he didn't get a response, he went around to the back and prised the door open, using an axe that Jessie had supplied.

Covering his face with a handkerchief, Robert followed closely behind as the constable entered. The smell was so intense that the constable had to turn back to the yard for fresh air.

Robert looked through the textured glass in the dining room door and could only make out a blurred image of what appeared to be a family sitting around the long dining room table. The sight was so frightening that he did not enter.

The constable returned a few minutes later and saw that there were four corpses tied to chairs around the table. He had not expected anything like this when he followed Robert to the Hamilton estate. Seconds later he used the house's telephone to call the police station for backup. Within ten minutes of this call the entire house was filled with police.

Robert was then taken to the police station where he gave a statement, before returning to the factory.

Detective Inspector Richard Crombie, an experienced police officer who was looking forward to his imminent retirement, was put in charge and he described the crime scene in his notes.

The air was putrid and the closer I got to the deceased, the worse it became. Each family member was placed around the dining room table, all dressed in their Sunday best and all in different stages of decomposition. From what I could gather, it looked as if they had died at different times.

Eric Hamilton was at the head of the table, a glass of sherry placed in his left hand that was raised by string attached to his shirt collar. It was as if he was about to make a toast. A carving knife was glued to his right hand with his fingers clutching the handle. It seemed as though the murderer was setting a scene only he could enjoy.

Kathleen sat next to her husband. Her eyes were propped open with toothpicks and she was turned slightly, as if she was gazing into her husband's eyes that were also held open with toothpicks. Her right hand appeared to be gently resting on his lap.

Kathleen Hamilton's mother Edna Larson and her youngest daughter Leah sat on the other side of the table. Both were propped up with pillows and both were holding crystal goblets with sherry still inside. Bizarre smiles caused by string that ran through their lips then tied to their ears, made it appear as if they were really enjoying their last meal together.

Ivy Small, Edna Larson's mother, was the only one that sat by the fireplace. She was found with a ball of knitting on her lap and, like Edna and Leah, she had a drink in her hand and her lips were turned upright, as if she was also being forced to smile.

The table was set with fine china. A large ham, which was being swarmed by flies when I arrived, was placed near Mr Hamilton, who appeared as though he was about to carve it.

A brightly coloured bowl filled with boiled potatoes and cabbage was placed beside the ham and buns filled a basket near a rather large pickle tray that was also being devoured by insects.

A white cloth covered the table and matching embroidered napkins were laid on the victims' knees, all neatly folded. An array of red candles that surrounded a vase full of dead red roses appeared to be the centrepiece.

After a thorough search of the home, the crime-scene photos were taken then all the bodies were removed to the mortuary. An autopsy would soon reveal the cause of death for each victim. Detective Inspector Crombie would learn two days later that the Hamilton's maid, who had arrived at the house some months before, was missing.

The neighbours, who knew the maid only by her given name, Elizabeth, stated that she hadn't been seen in several days. Detective Inspector Crombie immediately returned to the Hamilton estate, but he could find little evidence that she had ever lived there.

One of the neighbours, Bonney Clarkson, recounted how Eric Hamilton had been forced to give up his study to make room for the new maid. But the room was now back to its original state. Mr Hamilton's desk and his writing material were neatly placed under the east window and all of his books were back on the shelves. A small safe inside the closet revealed some documents and a large quantity of cash. It appeared as though nothing had been stolen.

The attic was filled with old clothing, an oversized trunk and various pieces of broken and discarded furniture. It looked as if no one had been there for several days. Dust filled the air and the smell of stale cigar smoke lingered in the room.

The detective now focused his attention on the Hamiltons' maid. The neighbours had said that Elizabeth had been hired by Kathleen, just a few months earlier. 'She was a lovely lass with a ready smile,' said Bonney Clarkson, a neighbour that lived a few doors down. Then she hesitated, as if she had more to say.

'Go on,' encouraged Detective Inspector Crombie.

'I overheard an argument between Mr and Mrs Hamilton on the day she arrived. Mrs Hamilton isn't– she wasn't a good housekeeper, and they often argued about that. And... other things. She moved her relations – the two old ladies, and her sister, Miss Larson – in without his permission and he didn't like that. But I didn't hear any disturbances since.'

The detective now worried that the maid may also have been a victim. 'What does she look like, this Elizabeth?'

Bonney described Elizabeth as a very pretty young girl, possibly seventeen or eighteen years of age, with long red curls and bright blue eyes. She also mentioned that she had a robust figure.

When he interviewed Mrs O'Donnell, who said she had spoken to the maid a few times, he discovered that she had lost both her parents years earlier. 'She didn't have a soul left in the world, detective,' said Mrs O'Donnell.

Sadly this was all the neighbours knew about Elizabeth and now the police were extremely concerned for her safety. They knew that the monster that had taken Eric, Kathleen, Edna, Leah and Ivy would never have left a witness behind.

As Detective Inspector Crombie painstakingly searched Eric Hamilton's home, he did notice something a little peculiar. Every cup, saucer and plate was lined up perfectly in the cupboards. Every tea towel, cloth and piece of linen was folded in a precise manner.

Considering what the neighbours had said about Kathleen's housekeeping skills, he expected to see a much more disorganised home. In the pantry, he also found the preserves neatly stacked according to the dates they had been bottled. Surely the maid hadn't been there long enough to do all these tasks and look after this large family.

It was strange, to say the least, but nothing about this led the officer any closer to the murderer. Now fearing that the maid was more likely dead than not, he ordered that the half acre surrounding the home be searched thoroughly, including the abandoned well behind the coach house. This would take at least a week to do.

In the meantime, the O'Donnells kindly looked after the horses and did their best to keep nosey onlookers from peering inside the Hamilton's windows.

Rumours about this gruesome discovery had circulated and before the week was up, the town of Briarwood was filled with people from the surrounding area, all hoping to get a look at where these dreadful murders had taken place.

Mr Hamilton's garment factory had been closed and all monies, including the payroll account were frozen during the investigation. All the employees were then asked to come in and give a statement and every one of them co-operated with the police. Two men, who freely admitted they didn't like Eric Hamilton, were interviewed several times, but were cleared of wrongdoing.

The O'Donnells' two sons were also brought in for questioning, but both had rock-solid alibis.

By the end of May, the officers had searched every square inch of the Hamilton property and had not found anything that would lead them to Elizabeth's whereabouts. She was the only person who hadn't been accounted for and Detective Inspector Crombie was beginning to wonder if she might have had something to do with these murders.

At the mortuary on the outskirts of town the bodies of each of the victims were being examined.

It was determined that Eric Hamilton had been the first one

to die. 'Hemlock poisoning,' said the medical examiner. 'It's a terrifying way to die. Paralysis sets in first, and the victim is alive for a while but unable to move.'

Kathleen had died within a few hours of her husband, she too, had been poisoned by hemlock.

Edna and Leah were also poisoned but the perpetrator had used strychnine and Ivy, Kathleen's grandmother, was smothered. 'See the way the tiny blood vessels in her eyes have ruptured?' said Doctor Lohan, the medical examiner to a repulsed Detective Inspector Crombie. The medical examiner could not determine the exact time of death, but did say based on decomposition that they all died within a few days of one another.

Murdering the head of the household first made sense, as Mr Hamilton could have overcome the killer. He stood five feet, ten inches and had a strong, muscular build. Eliminating the strongest member of the family first would have been the most logical thing to do.

The whole situation was highly unusual and there was no apparent motive. Nothing had been taken and even the money in Eric's wallet hadn't been touched. Whoever had done this was methodical and had taken their time.

It was also very possible that they were now looking at two individuals for this mass murder.

This case left many questions. Why hadn't the neighbours heard or seen anyone coming or going and why hadn't any of the victims called out for help? The medical examiner's findings suggested that the victims were probably given sedatives just prior to their deaths to keep them quiet and subdued.

Still, this didn't answer the question about the perpetrators: why had they not been seen?

Each of the victims may have believed they were just feeling poorly and had taken to their beds, hoping this would pass.

Crombie recalled the foreman, Robert Carlyle, reporting that Eric Hamilton said that he was ill. But he never mentioned anything about his wife or other family members. It was possible though. Perhaps Hamilton hadn't told his foreman anything more than he had to.

As the detective delved into Eric Hamilton's past, he could not find a soul that would have wanted to hurt him or his family. Eric, like most business-minded people, had sparked some jealousy from one of his competitors, but this was several years ago.

Although every effort to find the Hamilton's maid had failed, no one could say for certain if she had even been living in the home when the murders took place. The detective surmised that it was possible she had quit her job weeks earlier. The last time anyone had seen Elizabeth was on April 22.

Janet Crosby, another maid who worked two houses down from the Hamiltons, reported that she had seen her at the grocers on Brant Street. Elizabeth was there to pick up some flour and sugar. Miss Crosby remembered the date because the family she worked for were celebrating their fifteenth anniversary that night. When asked if Elizabeth seemed like herself, Miss Crosby replied, 'Oh yes, she was as lovely as ever and even asked if I would like to go to the Sunflower Tea Shop but I had to get back to look after the children.' She added, 'You know, I wouldn't have blamed that young lass for leaving that awful home because she had told me how Kathleen was constantly screaming orders at her and that she was never satisfied with anything she did for her or the rest of her family.'

The detective was now forming a picture in his mind of this conflicted family. Although no one really knew Mrs or Miss Larson, all the neighbours agreed that they were just as loud and miserable as Kathleen. Ivy, the grandmother, was rarely seen or heard from, because she had a litany of ailments that didn't allow her much freedom.

Detective Inspector Crombie was beginning to believe that Kathleen Hamilton may have been the original target of this heinous crime. Could her obnoxious and rather crass personality be responsible for the murders of her entire family?

2

As Detective Inspector Crombie studied the crime-scene photos, he couldn't help but wonder how someone had pulled this off without being seen or heard. Eric weighed twelve stone, so the perpetrator had to be a man of at least similar height and weight. How could such a person go unnoticed?

This killing would have taken some time and now he wasn't convinced that it had been done by just one person. Positioning the victims and setting the scene would have taken the strength of two average men, or a man and woman. And how long would it have taken? Then they'd left without a trace. *I've never seen anything like this before,* he thought. *It's as if the devil himself came into the Hamiltons' home and then disappeared into thin air.*

Without any witnesses or a description of anyone unusual in the neighbourhood in the days leading up to the discovery, a quick resolution looked unlikely. Crombie was working day and night, going over all the statements his men had collected from the neighbours, their friends and Mr Hamilton's employees. Without any further leads, he decided to pay another visit to the coroner's office.

The medical examiner's notes were unclear about the

victims' stomach contents and the detective wanted to examine the clothing they had been wearing when they were found. Doctor Lohan explained that there was nothing in their digestive tracts, indicating that they hadn't eaten in several days at time of death.

He did find something very unusual about how they had been presented. 'The women's nails were cut and shaped and their hair had been washed and set. Eric Hamilton had been shaved – possibly after he was dead – and his hair was also washed. I found remnants of lye soap at his neckline.' Lohan also noticed that the clothing they were wearing had been altered as the stitching was coming loose. 'Done in a hurry, I should say.'

Each woman was dressed in identical frocks, made from a readily available cotton. Kathleen, Edna, Leah and Ivy had been dressed after their death. 'Look at these tiny tears,' said Lohan. 'Rigor had begun to set in, so it was hard for our murderer to manoeuvre the limbs.'

Crombie nodded. 'He must have spent an awful lot of time at the crime scene.'

'Yes,' said Lohan. 'He certainly made sure it was staged perfectly.'

'What do you think about this, doctor?' Crombie asked. 'What point was the killer trying to make? If it was revenge, then why did he go to all the trouble of staging the family? Why not just kill them and be done with it?'

Doctor Lohan was silent for a moment, scrutinising Crombie as if he was trying to make up his mind. 'Have you come across a colleague of mine, Doctor Bertram Killam?'

Crombie knew of Doctor Killam. He had helped Scotland Yard solve the case of the Cider Valley Killer. Mortimer Giles had been hiding in plain sight for several years. After six women had been raped and murdered in London in 1910, the citizens living close to where the murders occurred began demanding answers. Doctor Killam had a look at the similarities in each case and he was later able to give a description of where the killer might live, what job he may have and whether he was a family man or a loner. Once this was established every man within a twenty-mile radius of the crimes and fitting his description was brought in for questioning. A month after the last attack Giles was captured. Without his help, Scotland Yard may never have solved these crimes.

With no further leads in the Briarwood murders, Detective Inspector Crombie convinced his superiors that Doctor Killam's services might be of vital importance in solving this case. As a professor of psychiatry who was now teaching his skills to others at a university in London his time would be limited, but the detective was desperate for any help he could offer.

On the morning of June 18, Detective Inspector Crombie anxiously awaited the doctor's arrival at Union Station, just outside Briarwood. Doctor Killam had said he preferred casual attire and to look for a man wearing a light-coloured waistcoat with no hat. After searching through the crowds getting off the 8am train, the detective saw no passenger who fit the description he had in the back of his mind.

But then a handsome young man dressed in light beige jacket and trousers introduced himself as Bertram. He told the detective he didn't like formalities and preferred to be called by his first name and then he asked for the detective's first name. Once the introductions were done, Bertram insisted that they enjoy breakfast at the railway hotel in Briarwood, before heading over to the scene of the crime at 68 Carlton Lane.

Bertram was not like any doctor that Richard had ever

known. He was confident, but not conceited and although some young women in the hotel were obviously attracted to this young man, he didn't seem to notice. His actions were somewhat animated and whenever there was a lull in the conversation, he whistled. Bertram told the detective that this was a nervous habit that he picked up during his university years. 'Helps me concentrate,' he added.

Despite his rather unusual personality, Crombie found him pleasant company and could see that he was extremely eager to help solve this mystery.

After breakfast, they headed over to the Hamilton estate. Bertram hopped out of the carriage the minute they arrived and then began walking around the property as the detective followed close behind.

A few minutes later, they entered the house and they were overcome by the foul smell that still lingered inside. The detective described where each of the deceased family members were found and how they were staged to look as though they were about to have dinner.

All the while, Bertram took notes. At one point he stopped suddenly, turned toward the window ledge and ran his finger across the surface. This seemed odd, but Crombie didn't question his reasons.

Once they were finished in the dining room, Bertram asked that the detective show him what room the maid was given. Although it had already been searched thoroughly, something caught the doctor's eye the minute he entered. A small gold earring was stuck in the carpet fibres.

The detective was very angry that this had been overlooked by his officers but Bertram insisted it was just an oversight. 'These things go unnoticed more often than you think. Don't worry yourself, old chap, I'm sure it wasn't done on purpose.'

Bertram began whistling as he crawled on his hands and

knees searching for the matching earring, but nothing more was found.

The doctor studied the fine detail in the earring. Once he was done, he placed it in his hand and said, 'This earring would have cost an average man a year's wages!'

'So it'll belong to the mistress then,' said Crombie, reasoning that a maid of Elizabeth's standing would never have been able to afford such a luxury. Bertram wasn't so sure, but decided it was best not to draw any conclusions, until he had gone over all the evidence.

After several hours at the Hamilton estate, the detective suggested they return to his office to see the crime-scene photos. On the way there Bertram asked several questions regarding what the neighbours had said about the maid. He was particularly interested in how Elizabeth had conducted herself when she was out in public.

This seemed odd to Detective Inspector Crombie as he really didn't consider her as a person of interest. Everything he had heard about Elizabeth had suggested that she was a lovely young girl, with a passive demeanour and a kind spirit.

Once they got back to the police station, Bertram was directed to the gruesome crime-scene photos that lined the walls of Detective Inspector Crombie's office. There was also a detailed map of the Hamilton's property and outbuildings.

As Bertram stood back and examined the photos, he began whistling again. A short time later, he asked for a magnifying glass to have a closer look. Crombie could see by his expression that he was puzzled about something he had seen.

A few minutes later the doctor said, 'A woman was definitely involved, but I believe that she may have had an accomplice.' He explained, 'Whoever did this is a true psychopath with little to no empathy for the victims. A woman who has psychotic tendencies is more likely to insist on perfection. Notice the way the table was set and how the victims were dressed. This is an indicator that the main suspect is the maid, Elizabeth. She is the only one that could have pulled this off.'

Crombie remained silent, waiting to see where this was going.

The doctor continued, 'She could enter and leave the Hamilton's home without being questioned, so she could take her time with each victim. I believe she gets a feeling of intense pleasure – euphoria if you will – from accomplishing certain tasks. To put it simply, she enjoys every part of this, from watching her victims die, to staging them. And disturbingly, I believe she is likely to do this again.'

The detective, who knew nothing about the troubled mind, replied, 'I have to say, sir, your conclusion seems a little premature. I mean, how can you look at a photo and decide who the killer or killers might be?'

Bertram laughed, then replied, 'Years of practice, my friend.' He then explained, 'Look carefully at this setting and you will notice that all eyes are looking toward Eric Hamilton. His wife, Kathleen, who you have said ruled the household, is now gazing up at her husband with her hand gently placed on his lap. Edna and Leah, who like Kathleen – according to the neighbours – showed little respect for Mr Hamilton, are now looking at him, smiling graciously as if they admired the man. And then there is poor old grandma Ivy placed in a comfortable chair, looking toward the head of the household and also smiling. Doesn't that say anything to you? Does this not suggest that our perpetrator was a woman?'

Detective Inspector Crombie now had a closer look at the photo. It suddenly became very clear to him. A man surely wouldn't have gone to all this trouble or taken the time to do all this – including cooking an entire meal and setting the table.

The Hamilton family who had been described by everyone who knew them as discordant, were now sitting down to a meal together, seemingly enjoying each other's company, with all the women looking at Eric Hamilton with admiration and goodwill.

The scene was so bizarre that Crombie could not imagine the maid described as demure was the killer. He had originally dismissed the possibility of a woman mainly because of the strength needed to move someone like Eric Hamilton.

'It wouldn't be an easy task,' Bertram agreed. 'She must have had help. A lover perhaps?'

A plan to go to the coroner's office the following day was in order, as Bertram wanted to have a good look at the clothing they were wearing when they were placed around the table. He did tell the detective, 'Finding the murderer will be a difficult task, as she had left the scene without being noticed and the home was cleaned from top to bottom, reducing the likelihood of finding any finger marks.'

After a long day, Bertram returned to the Railway Hotel. But instead of retiring for the night he went over his notes and each time he did, he drew the same conclusion. Now his only question was how had this young woman endured the odour produced by the decaying bodies for so long. Considering the effort it took to do this, the lengthy exposure to this dreadful smell would have been horrendous. Even for a cold-hearted killer, this would not have been an easy task. Although lime powder or vinegar and baking soda were sometimes used in the mortuary to decrease the smell, this would not have been of much help during the time that the victims were being staged.

Was it possible that it just didn't affect Elizabeth the way it affected most people?

After less than three hours' sleep Bertram arrived back at the police station long before Richard Crombie arose the following morning. He wanted to have one more look at the crime-scene photos before heading down to the coroner's office. When the detective arrived later that morning, several constables approached him to complain about Bertram's incessant whistling. Detective Inspector Crombie wasn't bothered by this, but the officers were certainly glad when the men left the police station later that morning.

Bertram now had less than three days to work through this case and with the pressure mounting to solve it, the detective allowed him free access to everything involving the Hamilton murders.

Of course, he couldn't solve it in this time but he could offer his opinion and allow the officers to do their job. He could also give a profile of the kind of person that would do such a crime. If his theory was correct it could save the officers time, resources and possibly more lives.

The corpses had decomposed further in storage but Bertram insisted on having a careful look at each one.

He then turned to the clothing, noticing that the same colour of thread used to alter the garments had been used to secure their mouths open. This may have been the last thing that the killer had done before leaving, as everything else was done using other materials, like the glue and the toothpicks.

Then he scanned a few of the reports that had been written about the deaths. The coroner's remarks about the sherry in the goblets caused him to raise an eyebrow. 'The goblets contained an excellent sherry. No bottle of sherry was discovered in the house, though bottles of whisky and ale were present.'

A few pages later he noted that Robert Carlyle, Eric's foreman, had stated that Mr Hamilton hated sherry, calling it liquid candy, only suitable for a child. This only cemented the doctor's theory that it was a woman who had done this, as sherry was commonly consumed by them.

∼

As they rode back to the station that afternoon, Bertram whistled softly. Detective Inspector Crombie gathered that the doctor was in deep thought and rather than disturb him, he remained quiet during their carriage ride.

About fifteen minutes later, Bertram turned to the detective and asked to return to the Hamilton's home for one last look around. He didn't tell Crombie what he was looking for, only that a piece of this mysterious puzzle was missing. He added, 'Even the most thoughtful plans are generally flawed and despite the killer's best effort, it is likely she had left something behind.'

The attic was the only room in the house that the officers had not searched extensively and the doctor wanted to have another look there. They asked the cabman to wait, which he did, among a gathering crowd.

'Ghouls,' said Crombie dismissively.

Bertram smiled disarmingly. 'It's normal. People have a morbid curiosity after a crime like this. But just the same, keep a lookout for anyone who doesn't fit in. Many murderers, especially psychopaths, often revisit their crime scenes. It's possible that Elizabeth – or her accomplice – will do the same.'

The air in the attic was thick with dust that afternoon, but the smell of rotting flesh wasn't as apparent as it had been downstairs. Bertram didn't waste any time and began slowly, methodically removing the boxes and loose clothing scattered about the room. He inspected each item carefully, then tossed it into the only corner of the room that was clear of debris.

The warm temperatures had made their task very difficult and after two hours, they stepped outside to get some fresh air. Mrs O'Donnell, who had been watching the house the entire time, came over with some tea for both of them... Although she was nosey, both men appreciated the gesture.

And even more than the tea, they appreciated some information she gave. 'Inspector, I forgot to tell your officer earlier... Back in April, late at night, I saw a young man, a stranger, standing on the porch, just there, late at night.' But because it was very dark, all she could say for certain about this fellow was that it wasn't Mr Hamilton. She assumed it was a friend of the family. When asked if she had seen him after that evening, she said she hadn't.

A few hours later the men left the Hamilton's home without finding any further evidence. Bertram had to get back to London the following day and with this in mind, he went back to his hotel room and began preparing a profile on the main suspect. The lengthy report would outline his reasons and hopefully give the officers some insight into this killer.

Early the next morning, he arrived at the police station and gave his report to Detective Inspector Crombie. The doctor then spent a few minutes alone with the detective before he headed to the railway station. 'Word to the wise, inspector. Send your men back to the Hamilton's house and have them go through the study again. I think you might find something that will tell you Elizabeth's last name: a ledger book, a receipt or possibly a note from his bank. Surely, a man like Eric Hamilton would have something written somewhere about this elusive woman.'

Shortly after speaking to Detective Inspector Crombie, the doctor left for London.

In an effort to convince some of his more sceptical officers that Doctor Bertram was onto something, Crombie read the conclusion of his report out loud: 'In my time working as a criminal psychiatrist, I have learned a great deal about the psychotic mind. Intuition along with extensive training and many hours spent with the criminally insane has allowed me to ascertain the skills needed to detect what others cannot.'

Some of the more cynical officers shuffled and coughed, but Crombie silenced them with a glare and continued. 'I believe the maid known only as Elizabeth has had a troubled past. She was either born without a soul, has experienced heartbreak or had been neglected throughout her formative years…

'I am not sure if she managed to commit this crime independently. However, I am always amazed at the strength and determination of this type of killer. I would not be entirely surprised to learn that she did, in fact, do this on her own. But do not let this stop your search for a second suspect.

'I suggest you begin your search by revisiting the neighbours. People who are in shock often forget the smallest details and they may have remembered something that they believe wouldn't be helpful to this case but possibly is. I am hoping they can give you some insight as to where Elizabeth might have gone. They are the only ones that have spoken to this girl and something she might have said could lead you in the right direction.'

The junior constables wilted visibly at the thought of interviewing more neighbours.

Crombie turned the page and read on. 'Elizabeth could have easily stolen several items of value from the Hamilton estate, but she chose not to. This generally means that acquisition of property wasn't a motive and that she may be well off. If she does have the means to travel, I suspect she will. I also believe that this girl is of higher-than-average intelligence and it is likely that she got some sort of macabre pleasure from doing this. No one should underestimate the maid known only as Elizabeth. She is a methodical, cold-blooded killer who managed to get away without raising suspicion.'

The doctor's knowledge and understanding of the main suspect would later prove to be invaluable and although Detective Inspector Crombie was sceptical about bringing in a criminal psychiatrist, he would later come to admire Doctor Killam and his chosen profession.

3

As Crombie's constables worked on finding any paper trail that would expose Elizabeth's last name, Mrs O'Donnell was brought into the station to give a more detailed description of the main suspect. She was the most reliable witness because her home was directly across from the Hamiltons' and she had spoken to Elizabeth more than the other witnesses had.

Mrs O'Donnell still refused to believe that the maid had anything to do with the murders but provided a fairly detailed description of her. 'Elizabeth stood a few inches taller than me, and I am five foot and one inch. She had lovely red curly hair and blue eyes. I can't say how long her hair is because she always kept it up in a bun. Her skin was flawless and – surprisingly for a redhead – she didn't have any freckles and I don't believe I ever saw her wearing rouge.'

When asked about the maid's mannerisms, Mrs O'Donnell said, 'She spoke with a thick Northern Irish accent but I believe she said she had moved to London when she was a child.' She added, 'For a girl of her standing, I was surprised to learn that she knew how to read and write.' When asked how she could be sure, she said, 'She showed me her shopping list then mentioned how Kathleen had spelled paraffin incorrectly.'

The detective then showed her the earring that Bertram had found in Mr Hamilton's office and asked if she had ever seen Elizabeth wearing this. Mrs O'Donnell confirmed that it was the match to the pair that she had seen the maid wearing the last time they spoke.

Before Mrs O'Donnell left, she sat with a police artist who made a drawing of the suspect according to the details she provided. Still, she couldn't believe that this young girl had committed such a dreadful crime and said, 'The Elizabeth I knew couldn't have possibly done this horrendous crime, I'm certain she had nothing to do with it.'

Two other neighbours were also brought in and they all gave similar stories, although their descriptions of Elizabeth varied slightly. One said she was about five foot seven with a robust figure and the other said she was just five foot three and quite slim.

An hour later, Mrs O'Donnell called in to speak to the detective. She wanted to let him know where she believed Elizabeth may have purchased the gold earrings. In a rather excitable voice, she said, 'You know, Detective Inspector Crombie, I was thinking about this all the way home, and although there are many jewellers in London, there is one particular store on King Street that is known for their exquisite designs, just like the one Elizabeth left behind. It's called Stanley's and it has been there for as long as I can remember. Maybe, you can find Elizabeth's surname there: remember she did say that she had lived in London.'

This neighbour had given the detective the first piece of solid evidence that might lead him to the last name of this elusive maid. Unfortunately, his officers had not found one piece of evidence in the Hamilton home that would reveal it.

Time wasn't on the detective's side: Bertram's warning that she would kill again if not caught rang in his ears. With this in mind, the detective made plans to leave for London the following day. If he could get the maid's family name, he was certain he could find her.

Prior to leaving for London, he had enlisted the help of the newspapers and by the following day, a detailed description, which included a sketch of their main suspect, was printed in the *Briarwood News* and several London papers with a caption that read, *Do you know this girl?* Posters were also placed at all railway stations and inside the local post offices. A fifty-pound reward was offered for any information leading to the suspect's arrest.

It was now the beginning of July and the police were being pressured by the mayor to solve the grisly Hamilton family murders. This was completely understandable as the residents of this quiet town had never seen anything like this before.

The police remained vigilant and just a day after the newspaper articles were printed, three women fitting Elizabeth's description were brought into the police station. Each one was questioned extensively and released a short time later. All of these women had an alibi and people that could back up their statements. Several more women fitting Elizabeth's description would follow, but none could be linked to the Hamilton murders.

In the meantime, Detective Inspector Crombie left for London, hoping he would be able to gather the information he needed. His trip to London should have taken two-and-a-half days. Unfortunately, this wouldn't be the case as when he finally found Stanley's Jeweller's he was told that the owner, Mr Stein, was away on business, but would see the detective on his return. This would extend the trip to four days.

On the morning of July 4, Detective Inspector Crombie

impatiently sat in the waiting area of Stanley's Jewellery. The store clerk told the detective that Mr Stein was on the phone with a very important customer and couldn't be disturbed. Detective Inspector Crombie had never been in such a place. The walls were adorned with art and the jewels were kept under heavy tempered glass and accessible only with a key.

To lessen his discomfort while he waited, the detective was served tea and biscuits and given some magazines to read. However, forty-five minutes later, his patience was running out. He eventually flashed his warrant at the clerk and insisted he fetch the jeweller immediately. Another ten minutes went by before Mr Stein finally stepped into the waiting area.

At first, he seemed annoyed: the detective, who was dressed in a plain brown suit that smelled of stale cigar smoke, did not look like the clientele he was accustomed to. It was obvious to Mr Stein that this man could not afford to purchase anything from his store.

It wasn't until Detective Inspector Crombie introduced himself and explained why he was there that the jeweller began to soften and invited him into his office. He then demanded that his clerk bring them some fresh coffee.

'Thank you for seeing me today, Mr Stein,' said the detective. 'I'm here because I want your opinion on an earring found at a crime scene.'

This seemed to pique Mr Stein's interest and the moment the detective produced the earring, a smile came over the jeweller's face. He then placed the earring on a black velvet cloth, put on his spectacles and examined it for several moments. After handing it back to the detective he said, 'I'm afraid it wasn't me, but I do believe my late father may have made this. It is an exquisite piece of jewellery: just look at that detail.'

The detective then asked, 'Is there any way we could find out who may have purchased these earrings?'

Mr Stein thought about this for a moment, then replied, 'If my father did design this, I am certain I will be able to find the purchaser's name in his customer ledger.'

While Mr Stein was gone, Detective Inspector Crombie had a look at a silver pocket watch in one of the display cases. It was a handsome piece, but when he learned the price of it, he quickly changed his mind about the purchase.

A few minutes later, the jeweller returned with a large, dusty ledger book which also contained drawings of all the designs of the earrings sold between 1903 and 1908, the year Mr Stein senior passed away. After looking over each entry carefully, he found the design of the earring that the detective was inquiring about. Between 1903 and 1908, there had been four pairs sold to Mrs Helen Jester, Mrs Laura Archibald, Mrs Collette Forman and Mrs Silvia Riley.

Mr Stein did not have the addresses or contact information for any of them. Only their names appeared beside the order they had placed. He confessed to the detective that he had stopped offering that particular earring because he didn't have the same skill as his father where detail was concerned.

After writing the names down in his notes, Detective Inspector Crombie thanked Mr Stein for his time and headed to the post office to see if these women still lived in the area. Only one of them, Mrs Archibald, was still living in London, in an upmarket area of Finchley. But during a visit to her home the following day the detective determined that she was not connected to the Briarwood maid. In fact, she had no children of her own.

Regrettably, the detective could not find the other women on the list and although he continued to investigate every lead when he returned to Briarwood, he reached a dead end. With no further evidence, the case soon went cold.

As higher than normal temperatures hit the Briarwood area that summer, the coroner began to insist that the deceased Hamilton family be buried. All efforts had been made to locate their relatives since they were murdered, but no one came forward. Eric Hamilton had purchased a plot for him and his wife, offering each of them a lovely spot to rest under the canopy of a large willow tree in Elgin Memorial Gardens. Sadly, the other family members didn't fare so well and would end up in a common grave at the Union Cemetery.

By August of that same year, the horrible events that took place on Carlton Lane were finally becoming a faded memory for the townsfolk.

Although Detective Inspector Crombie still kept this case open, he had to move on to other more current cases. Whoever had killed the Hamilton family had seemingly gotten away with murder. No further information or sightings came into the police station and the detective also hit a dead end with the names of the women that had purchased the earrings. If they had lived in London at one time, they were not there now.

It was very hard for the detective to accept the outcome of this case and he certainly didn't know how this maid, known as Elizabeth, had come into town, secured a job, murdered five people and left without a trace. Without a last name or even one solid lead, it was becoming impossible to find her.

The other officers in his command began to complain that they were disturbed by the macabre crime-scene photos of the Hamilton family murders that were still on the board behind Detective Inspector Crombie's desk. The chief constable had a quiet word: 'Take them down, lad.' Subsequently they were packed inside an evidence box marked simply '68 Carlton Lane' to remain out of sight. But this mass murder would still be in the forefront of the detective's mind. He just couldn't accept that he had not been able to solve the most gruesome murder that he had ever been a party to.

After catching up on the work he had neglected during the investigation, Detective Inspector Crombie considered taking some time off to visit his ageing parents in Manchester. They were constantly inviting him over to their home, but something always got in the way and soon a letter would arrive from Doctor Killam that would postpone this visit too.

Bertram had sent an article he found in an old psychiatric periodical. The article, titled, 'The Disturbed Mind of a Child', was about a young girl with the initials E.R., aged fourteen years, six months at the time the article was published. She had been found, aged twelve, with the bodies of her deceased parents on Christmas morning of 1907, in an upmarket neighbourhood near Kensington. A concerned neighbour had not seen the family at church the previous Sunday nor had they showed up for a gathering on Christmas Eve.

When police arrived, they had found the child in the kitchen making biscuits and acting as if everything was all right. Her parents, very obviously deceased, had been placed at the kitchen table and were dressed for a formal dinner party. Their mouths had been sewn into bizarre smiles and – like the Hamilton family – E.R.'s father was holding a goblet of sherry in his hand. A partially-eaten goose sat in the centre of the table surrounded by stewed prunes.

E.R. didn't seem to be bothered by the putrid smell and when she was told she had to come down to the station, she cheerfully put her coat and hat on and followed the officers out of the door.

The child was questioned extensively and it was obvious from the beginning that she didn't understand the seriousness of the charges brought against her. Her demeanour was recorded as being quite odd. She laughed inappropriately when she was questioned about the deaths of her mother and father. She also vehemently denied that someone had helped her, despite her slight build and her father's weight of ten stone.

E.R. showed no emotion during her trial and was later charged as an adult for murder. E.R.'s grandmother and only living relative, Marian Crawford was terrified that her granddaughter could be sentenced to hang and immediately instructed her solicitor that no expense was to be spared. The solicitor instructed an excellent barrister, who in turn instructed a dozen psychiatrists.

Every psychiatrist consulted about the case – including the one for the prosecutor – testified that the defendant was not of sound mind and wasn't responsible for what she had done. From that point on, the child would not spend another day in prison as she was transferred to a psychiatric hospital.

When E.R. turned sixteen, a little less than four years later, Mrs Crawford appealed her conviction and brought in more psychiatrists. During her appeal, they would tell the judge a long, convoluted story about how this young woman had changed dramatically and had made a sudden and miraculous recovery. They all recommended that E.R. be released from the psychiatric hospital and be placed into her grandmother's care. Three months later, E.R. was sent to live with her grandmother who died of heart failure three weeks before her granddaughter's seventeenth birthday. Mrs Crawford's will bequeathed all of her worldly goods to her granddaughter, amounting to a very sizeable inheritance.

A brief summary by Doctor Frederick Neil, the psychiatrist for the prosecution, was attached to the periodical. Crombie read it with interest, particularly noting one section:

I met with E.R. this morning and asked her directly if she had murdered her parents. She didn't hesitate when she replied, 'Yes, sir.'

My next question was also direct and I asked, 'Why did you murder your parents?'

She responded, 'I really don't know, but they did argue a lot, maybe that's why.'

I then asked, 'Do you think they suffered during the few days it took for the poison to take effect?'

E.R. began laughing and then said, 'I suppose so.'

I must admit, E.R. was a very curious case and I really couldn't say that I have ever interviewed anyone quite like her. At our next session, I tried to question her about an accomplice and at that point she simply sat back with a cold stare, folded her arms and refused to answer any further questions.

To conclude, during our brief time together, I noticed that E.R. was of higher intelligence and that she had the mannerisms of someone with a high social standing. I believe that this young girl could fool others into believing that she is also of high moral standing, a Christian perhaps, and someone that could not possibly do the things she was accused of. Her stare is generally blank and her expressions do not change regardless of the topic being discussed.

Alarmingly, I do think this child is capable of committing further acts of violence and I cannot express strongly enough that she should remain within the walls of the psychiatric hospital for the remainder of her life and be monitored closely.

Bertram added a short note addressed to Detective Inspector Crombie:

I do believe this girl could be the Elizabeth you are looking for. You should be able to ascertain the name of her mother and father if you can find the police report from the 1907 Kensington murders. Elizabeth may have had another psychiatric breakdown after her grandmother's death in 1910, precipitating the Hamilton family murders. I hope that this will lead you to your suspect.

4

The trip Richard was planning to take to see his elderly parents was once again postponed. But it seemed that by doing a little more research into Elizabeth's background, it could lead to her last name and possible arrest. This gave him and his officers the motivation to reopen this case. If not for Dr Bertram Killam's keen eye and willingness to help, he may never have known anything more about the Hamiltons' maid.

After contacting the Metropolitan Police about the murders that had taken place on Christmas morning of 1907, the detective ascertained his suspect's last name: it was Riley.

Elizabeth's father, Andrew Riley, was a skilled surgeon and had worked at the St. Thomas' Hospital in London for fifteen years. Andrew was forty-one when he was murdered and his wife, Sylvia, was thirty-seven. Elizabeth was their only child.

During a brief trip to Kensington, Detective Inspector Crombie learned from some of his colleagues in the Met that Andrew Riley had adored his daughter, but he was terribly worried about her constant outbursts. The Met detectives suggested he talk with a nurse who had worked alongside the surgeon for fifteen years. She told Crombie, 'Elizabeth never came to the surgery to see her father but I was told she was a wicked child, who often had to be restrained to keep her from hurting her own mother.'

When the detective asked about the Rileys' friends she said, 'Sadly, because of their daughter's temper, they generally kept to themselves, but occasionally Andrew would talk about spending time with his neighbour, Doctor Steven O'Leary.'

The nurse had been very helpful and as the detective made his way to Doctor O'Leary's home, he was ill-prepared for what he would uncover. It was a lovely October day and as he passed the beautifully-manicured gardens and lovely homes similar to the house where Elizabeth had once lived, he wondered why a child that seemingly had everything a young girl could ask for would murder her own mother and father.

When he reached 173 Campden Hill, he marvelled at the grand home the Rileys had once lived in. A cobbled path led to their oversized porch that was adorned with potted marigolds, a lovely white, cast-iron table and two matching chairs. The atmosphere was very inviting and the detective just couldn't imagine how a grisly murder could have ever taken place there. A few hundred feet from the Riley's home was Doctor Steven O'Leary's residence.

Now hoping to get some insight into the Riley family, notably Elizabeth, the detective rang the bell and was quickly greeted by the doctor's maid, who instructed him to wait in the parlour. The parlour was warm and cosy and as he waited for Doctor O'Leary, the detective couldn't help but notice the two noisy parakeets singing and chattering in an oversized cage by the window.

About five minutes later the maid returned with a pot of tea and biscuits. Doctor O'Leary arrived soon after. He was not exactly what the detective was expecting.

The elderly man, who quickly announced that he had just

celebrated his ninetieth birthday, greeted the officer with a strong handshake. Once the maid had helped him into his chair, he sat back, smiled at the detective, lit his pipe and said, 'What can I do for you, sir? I am certain that you didn't make this trip just to come and see an old man.'

Detective Inspector Crombie was forthcoming and asked what, if anything, he could tell him about the Riley family, specifically Elizabeth.

Doctor O'Leary turned to his maid and asked her to bring them in two glasses of his finest whisky. When she had left the room he remarked, 'The last time I talked about this was to my wife and that was at least three years ago.' After a short pause, he began to tell the detective his thoughts about this family. 'First, Detective Inspector Crombie, you have to understand that Sylvia really never wanted children. It was Andrew that insisted they at least try, but she was adamant that her body was too frail to produce an offspring. Sylvia was a delicate woman, always taken to her bed for one illness or another and when she found herself heavy with child, her whole personality changed. I am not saying she was not a likeable person but something snapped in her and she took on an entirely different persona. This strange personality trait seemed to have been passed down to Elizabeth tenfold. This child was not like most and you could tell that there was something odd about her from the moment she could communicate and as she grew older, I can honestly say, my wife and I were a little frightened by her at times.'

Crombie looked carefully at the older man. 'I am really not sure what you mean, doctor. Do you think she might have been born this way?'

Doctor O'Leary drank his whisky and asked for another. It was as if he was finding this part of his life difficult to relive. A few minutes later he said, 'To understand Elizabeth you would have to have met her. She just seemed as though she was living

Finding Elizabeth

in her own world, one that was cold and uncaring. The way she would stare at you, always watching your every movement with little to no expression. In fact, I couldn't tell if I ever saw that child smile. By the time Elizabeth was ten, Andrew Riley admitted to me that he and his wife had begun to lock their bedroom door at night. Can you imagine how frightening it would be, to fear your own child?'

Doctor O'Leary looked thoughtfully through the window for a moment before saying, 'You know, I was not surprised to hear she had murdered her parents, but the way she displayed them was ungodly.' He drew a shaky breath. 'This was certainly a tragedy that could have been prevented. If only Andrew had placed her into an asylum, like I suggested, they might still be alive today.'

A few minutes later another whisky arrived. As Dr O'Leary looked over at a photo of his wife, he smiled and said, 'My wife meant the world to me but I never blamed Andrew for his indiscretions. I think that dealing with a hysterical wife and a psychotic child left him feeling exhausted most days, but thankfully Elizabeth has no siblings and Andrew's parents had died long before that horrid child was born.'

Doctor O'Leary had no idea where Elizabeth might be now, but he was very thankful that the child's grandmother had put the Rileys' home up for sale shortly after the murders, adding, 'The new family brought life back into that home.'

Doctor O'Leary also said that the coroner who performed the autopsies on Andrew and Sylvia had concluded that the deceased had an excessive amount of arsenic in their bloodstreams. 'It was much higher than the lethal dose,' explained the doctor. 'It would have resulted in a most unpleasant death.'

Although the detective still had trouble believing that Elizabeth acted alone during the Hamilton murders, he was coming to terms with the possibility. Having one person with her psychopathic traits was unusual, but two seemed highly unlikely.

Now armed with this information, the detective headed back to Briarwood to give his officers an update. Elizabeth Riley's name and a more detailed description was sent to every police station within a fifty-mile radius of Briarwood, and it wasn't long before he received information from an officer in Leeds, regarding a young woman who fitted his suspect's description.

A cab driver there said he had picked Elizabeth up at the railway station the previous day and had taken her to the Sunrise Inn on Admiral Street. He also mentioned that he didn't think she would be staying at the inn for more than a few days, because she travelled so lightly.

This was exactly what the police in Briarwood had hoped for and as Crombie awaited a call from the detectives in Leeds, he contacted Bertram to tell him an arrest was imminent.

Bertram was relieved as he had read the details of Elizabeth Riley's time in the psychiatric hospital and found some disturbing revelations. The psychiatrists that Elizabeth's grandmother had paid handsomely to examine her granddaughter and later state that Elizabeth was cured, were complete frauds. Mrs Crawford had been swindled out of hundreds of pounds by three stage actors with absolutely no knowledge of the psychotic mind. Elizabeth had not been cured and in reality, she had been diagnosed as incurable by the head of psychiatry and two of his associates.

As a professor of criminal psychiatry, Bertram was extremely interested in what motivated Elizabeth to do such dreadful things and he hoped that one day he would have a chance to interview her. He had interviewed many sequential killers, but none of them came close to Elizabeth Riley. No, she was completely different from the rest and although they had murdered and tortured their victims, none had ever gone to the trouble of staging them.

Detective Inspector Crombie told Bertram that it was probable the prosecutor would want a thorough psychiatric evaluation and then said he would recommend him when the time came. Both men, for different reasons, were very curious about what went on inside the mind of this disturbed woman.

The officers at Briarwood held their collective breath, as they awaited the news from Leeds City Police that Elizabeth Riley had been arrested. The last Detective Inspector Crombie had heard, was that they had surrounded the inn. As far as the innkeeper knew, Elizabeth was in her room and hadn't come down for breakfast. She had not tried to hide her identity and had even signed the registry, E. Riley. After evacuating the rest of the inn, the officers attempted to go inside her room, on the second floor.

To their surprise, the door was ajar, but they found the room empty. The bed hadn't been slept in and there was no sign that she had even been there. A thorough search didn't offer any further clues to her whereabouts.

No one had seen her leave and the innkeeper swore she had checked in the previous day and had ordered food to be brought to her room.

Ronald Carlton, who had driven her to the inn in his cab stated, 'I saw a young woman waving her arms and I realised she was looking for a taxi. She asked if I could recommend a hotel and I told her about the Sunrise Inn. She smiled and handed me a half crown then asked that I take her there. The fare was only ten pence but she insisted I keep the change. Something about her was familiar and as I was helping her with her bag, I realised she was the woman in the police *wanted* posters.'

Mr Carlton then gave a detailed description of what she was

wearing and also mentioned that she spoke with a Northern Irish accent.

Although she had disappeared once again, the Leeds police were relatively confident, but not a hundred per cent certain, that they would make an arrest before day's end. This was unsettling news for Detective Inspector Crombie, who had already told several people, including a reporter, that the Briarwood killer's arrest was imminent.

At the end of the day, without any further sightings, the detective decided to go to Leeds to help with the search. Once Elizabeth was found, she would have to be escorted back to Briarwood and he planned to do this himself.

The next morning, Detective Inspector Crombie arrived in Leeds and was greeted by Detective Sergeant Bowman of Leeds City Police, who quickly gave him an update on their search for Elizabeth. 'We haven't got her,' said Bowman. 'But she can't have got far. No one's helping her in this city.'

Their first stop was the inn, where Detective Inspector Crombie confirmed that Elizabeth Riley had checked in and did in fact order tea and apple crumble cake to her room that same afternoon.

The innkeeper, a Mr Clark, remarked that the posters were a good likeness. 'She was a little thinner though,' he added.

'What about her demeanour?' asked Crombie.

'She was a rather sweet young lady and when she paid for her room in advance she gave me an extra ten pence for carrying her bag upstairs.'

Nothing about Elizabeth made the innkeeper think that she could be a murderer. In fact, he was completely taken aback when he heard what she had done in Briarwood. Now the only question left to answer was where had she gone from here?

By checking the room she had been staying in, Detective Inspector Crombie determined that she had slept in the bed but had remade it prior to leaving that morning. She had also taken a bath, as the bath salts supplied by the inn had been opened.

'What do you make of it?' asked Detective Sergeant Bowman.

Crombie ran a finger along the edge of the bath. 'She left the Briarwood crime scene immaculate too. Doctor Killam says it's a...' He paused, trying to remember the psychiatrist's term. 'A compulsive trait of hers.'

Still, this didn't answer his question as to when she left the inn or where she might have gone.

Mr Clark, who also lived on the premises, said he did not hear or see Elizabeth after she checked in except for when he delivered her tea. For all they knew, she could have left unnoticed in the middle of the night. If this was the case, she could have easily reached the edge of town without being seen.

On October 22, the detective reluctantly returned to Briarwood, without Elizabeth Riley. The search of this town and surrounding area did not give any further clues as to where she might have gone. All railway stations had been alerted and no one had reported any further sightings.

Her expensive attire might have given her identity away, and perhaps her London mannerisms, but now Crombie was beginning to think that she could fit in anywhere without being noticed. From a small town like Briarwood, to an urban centre, like Leeds. As he sat on the train that afternoon, he looked over his notes and saw that Mr Clark had said that Elizabeth was very polite and cordial. 'Nothing about this young lady stood out, she just seemed like any of my other female guests. The only thing I thought was a bit unusual was the fact that she was very young and travelling without a companion.'

Thinking back to what Bertram had said, Crombie was beginning to believe that Elizabeth was much more cunning than he once thought. She must have known that the taxi driver had recognised her and she also knew that it would take some time for the officers to arrive.

Bertram had also said, 'Don't underestimate this young woman. I truly believe she is a master of manipulation.' He had also told Crombie that there was a fine line between insanity and higher intelligence. Committing such acts and getting away with it took a lot of time and planning. The detective knew that the average killer would have made a series of mistakes, left clues behind and been caught long before this. Yes, Elizabeth was very cunning and meticulous. She had murdered the entire Hamilton family and although she accidentally left her earring behind, she had made sure that she got rid of any evidence that might lead the police to her and now the detective knew that she was in control and not the other way around.

Bertram had called during his absence to see if Elizabeth had been picked up, anxious to hear if she had been arrested without incident. Crombie returned his call and, with some embarrassment for his previous zealous confidence about what he thought would be a simple arrest, he explained what had happened.

The constable who had taken Bertram's original call had told the doctor that Elizabeth had not been captured. 'It is disappointing,' said the doctor to his detective friend. 'But you are not to blame.' He had done some thinking over the last few days and now believed that Elizabeth may have actually liked the challenge and the thrill of getting away without being noticed and eluding capture.

Crombie took the doctor's words in, and realising there was more to come, stayed silent.

Bertram continued, 'This thrill may encourage her to commit another horrendous act, particularly if she believes she could get away with it again.'

This certainly wasn't what the detective wanted to hear. If

Bertram was right, Elizabeth could already be looking for her next victims.

Bertram said, 'The mind of a psychotic killer is like no other. They are either born evil or become evil by some underlying factors during their adolescence. Even I know that psychoanalysis is flawed and that more often than I like to believe, the best psychiatrists can be manipulated by a true psychopath.'

Armed with this new information, Detective Inspector Crombie revised his plan. If this were true, Elizabeth would be much harder to apprehend than he had thought.

She was financially stable, having been left a large inheritance, and able to travel throughout the British Isles very easily. But an examination of her financial affairs and banking history revealed a surprise. It seemed that any money she once had was not being held in a bank account or trust company, although it was inconceivable that a woman would travel carrying the kind of money Elizabeth Riley's grandmother had left her, and now Crombie realised that there was only one conclusion.

She's entrusted someone with her fortune, he thought. *She has an accomplice.*

Now without any clues as to who that might be, the detective continued to concentrate on finding Elizabeth before she killed again.

5

Elizabeth grew up in one of the better areas of London and this is where Bertram and Detective Inspector Crombie assumed she would be heading back to.

As Scotland Yard kept a close eye on the Kensington neighbourhood, Elizabeth was searching for a room to let, just east of Preston, Lancashire, in the market town of Chester.

Elizabeth prided herself on her mastery of other dialects. So it was easy for her to fit in unnoticed. She had also changed her appearance, having cut her hair, changing the style completely. And she had abandoned her fine clothes for garments more suitable for this rural community.

Now she looked completely different from the young woman that the innkeeper in Leeds had described and no one questioned this lass when she arrived. Within a few days, she had convinced the owners of a boarding house that she had lost her parents in a dreadful fire. 'I just need a quiet place to stay while I wait for my grandmother to take me back to Manchester,' she told Frank Walker and his wife Patty. And the kindly couple agreed to let a room to who they thought was an unfortunate orphan.

Meanwhile, back in Briarwood, the case involving the Hamilton family murders grew cold again and the detective gave in to pressure and returned to the work he had been neglecting. His first case involved a bank manager that had been embezzling money from his customers. To a man who valued excitement the drudgery of trailing through closely-written financial records was close to torture.

As November arrived, nothing much had changed. Elizabeth Riley had disappeared again and no one had been able to apprehend her.

Sadly, during the time that Detective Inspector Crombie had spent trying to find his suspect, both of his elderly parents died from consumption. Now feeling an enormous amount of guilt and being unable to concentrate at work, the detective took a much-needed break and spent the next two weeks at home. Alone with his thoughts, he couldn't help but blame himself for not being with them when they died.

Richard had felt this loss just two years earlier, when his wife of thirty years took ill and died before he could get to the hospital to be with her.

As he dealt with his grief and the tragic loss of his parents, Elizabeth was busy setting the scene of a double murder that had taken the lives of her new landlord Frank Walker and his wife Patty. Elizabeth was blissfully going about her business, without a care in the world, just hours after this lovely couple took their last breaths.

Once she removed a sign that offered rooms to let in their home, she purchased some provisions. She then spent a few more days with the deceased enjoying the peace and quiet that was now almost deafening in the Walker household.

Back in Briarwood, a major snowfall brought the town to its knees at the start of December.

Richard Crombie was finally coming to terms with his loss and beginning to realise that he was not responsible for the untimely death of his parents. Since moving to Briarwood with his wife, he had done everything in his power to convince his mother and father that they should join him there, even offering to move them into his home. Regrettably, his father, Jack Crombie, had been fiercely independent and like his son, he rarely asked for or even wanted the help available to him. They were gone and although Richard would miss them terribly, he knew they had lived long, full lives.

By mid-December, still unaware of what had taken place in Chester, Richard went back to work to fulfil his final six-month commitment before his retirement in May of 1913.

Two days later, Constable Mark Copeland dropped a newspaper on the detective's desk with a headline that read, '*Macabre discovery shocks the residents of Chester*'. The description of these murders was far too familiar and the detective knew straight away that Elizabeth Riley had to be the prime suspect.

The home where the Walkers had lived a rather quiet life was now another bizarre crime scene. The couple that once rented out a room or two hadn't been missed for almost two weeks and if not for their regular coal delivery, their bodies might not have been found until the spring.

The familiar smell of decay was the first thing the officers noticed.

In the tiny parlour sat Patty Walker. She appeared as though she was about to read a book. Dressed in a plain white frock and multicoloured shawl, she sat by a large window that overlooked their garden. Her eyes had been forced open with toothpicks and the fingers of her right hand were glued to a book titled *Murder and Mayhem* that was on her lap. Her left hand was propped up with a pillow and her head was tilted towards it to look as if she was leaning on it. Her lips were sewn shut with coloured thread and turned down, as if she was frowning or displeased with something. Her legs were tied together so tightly with rope that her ankles were left with permanent indentations. The bruising and the way the blood had pooled suggested this had been done before her death.

Frank Walker didn't fare as well. He was found leaning up against the front desk where he would conduct his business. A leather strap secured over his arms and attached to either side of the desk with nails held him in place.

His eyes were also forced open and his lips were sewn upwards with thick white thread that was also sewn through his ear lobes. This made him appear as if he was smiling. For reasons only known to Elizabeth, his teeth had been extracted and placed into his hands with his fingers glued shut around them.

Blood from the extractions could be seen on his lips and shirt collar, which meant he might still have been alive too, but unconscious, when this was performed.

Although the body of Frank Walker was dressed from the waist up, he was missing his trousers and undergarments. This could have meant that Elizabeth was rushed, but Bertram would later surmise that this is exactly how she wanted him to be found.

Bertram felt that she truly enjoyed what she was doing and wanted to make some sort of a statement about Frank Walker who was said to be a flirt at times.

Detective Inspector Crombie offered his assistance and was

flatly turned down. Detectives from Scotland Yard had now taken over the case and Elizabeth Riley was put on their most wanted list. Although the Hamilton murders had not ended with an arrest, it was Richard that had retrieved crucial information regarding their prime suspect. Extremely frustrated by Scotland Yard's attempt to shut him out of the investigation, the detective did something no one saw coming: he retired in protest.

His officers would later say that they believed his pride got in the way. Detective Sergeant Cross, who was only thirty-four at the time, was quickly promoted to detective inspector.

Meanwhile, back in Chester, officers from as far away as London scoured the Walker home for clues – but Elizabeth had made sure that the home was left in perfect order and that any trace of her was long gone. Her room on the second floor was exactly the same as it had been when she arrived. Nothing had been disturbed. It didn't look as if she had ever slept in the bed or used the adjoining bathroom.

An autopsy was not able to pinpoint the exact time of death, but the coroner surmised that the couple had died within hours of one another. Tissue samples taken from the corpses confirmed that they had been poisoned with strychnine, a common rat poison.

Crombie in retirement smirked when he read an article about Scotland Yard's inability to capture Elizabeth Riley. They had been so certain that she would be caught that they told a reporter from *The Times* that her arrest was imminent. He remembered he had made the same error when they came close to arresting Elizabeth Riley in Leeds.

Richard Crombie knew that Elizabeth would outsmart them, just as she had outsmarted the Briarwood police officers and like Bertram, he believed that Elizabeth would simply move on to another unsuspecting family.

A week into their investigation, the Scotland Yard detectives had several false leads and they had spent a great deal of time questioning five girls fitting Elizabeth's description. Each one was eventually released without charge.

Now Scotland Yard was feeling the sting of their frightened citizens. If not for their foolish and premature statement to the press regarding Elizabeth's arrest, they would have been left alone and not felt as much pressure from the public.

As each day passed, the uproar grew and the Chester residents demanded to know why this young girl had not been apprehended. Elizabeth Riley had, once again, vanished without a trace and now everyone from Chester to London feared that they might be her next victim.

A huge amount of time and resources had gone into tracing Elizabeth, yet no one could say for sure where she might have gone. The Walkers had been dead for over a week when their bodies had been discovered, giving her ample time to leave the area without ringing any alarm bells.

During the investigation, all sightings of Elizabeth Riley were thoroughly followed up. By the end of December, the cost of finding their suspect had skyrocketed and now Scotland Yard was faced with a dilemma: either concede defeat or find more resources to put into the search.

The detectives from London were being stretched thin, as there were several unrelated murders being investigated in London. Many prostitutes had been found dead along the Thames. Although the police often looked the other way when prostitutes were assaulted, they could not ignore these gruesome murders.

The main suspect was a prominent figure in the community. His name was Kenneth Lawson and he was a highly respected civil engineer. His initials could be found on the Westminster bridge in Kensington along with various other structures all over Great Britain. Mr Lawson was also known to frequent the brothels and by all accounts, he was considered a generous man. He was a handsome chap who could have had his choice of women, but he preferred the most vulnerable and subservient. He once told a friend, 'The women of today are only interested in controlling their husbands, taking their money and flaunting their wealth. I have no desire to feed their egos, or their bellies.'

All evidence for the murders pointed to Kenneth Lawson, but his high-priced lawyer would never allow him to be interrogated alone. Maria Sarus, an experienced prostitute, told police 'Mr Lawson was the last one seen with seventeen-year-old Abbey Coulter before she disappeared.' Miss Coulter's body was later found face down in the river on 10 January.

Two days later Shawna Vanguard's body was found nearby. Like Abbey Coulter, she had been strangled.

Kenneth Lawson's lawyer denied all allegations against his client, even offering a vague alibi. He stated that on January 9, 10 and 12 Kenneth had been away on business in North Devon. Police didn't believe a word of it, but they couldn't make an arrest, since his alibi had been corroborated by his uncle, Stan Lawson.

When officers began following Kenneth Lawson on 15 January, his lawyer complained of an intrusion of privacy and they were instructed to stay out of sight. Since he had become their prime suspect and been kept under constant watch, no one else had been killed. Scotland Yard was certain they had the right man and they also knew that sooner or later he would seek out a prostitute's company.

So because the Met was overwhelmed by the crimes haunting the streets of London, Elizabeth Riley's case got pushed back. None of the leads that had come in after the

Walker murders had amounted to anything but a waste of time for Scotland Yard.

As February arrived and the long cold winter kept many people inside, the search for Elizabeth Riley came to an end.

As the police in Yorkshire had, the officers at Scotland Yard also underestimated her abilities. The posters that once lined every railway station, port and post office were fading along with any hope of ever finding her.

Elizabeth had once again changed her hairstyle and the clothes she wore, making it much easier for her to hide in plain sight. She was also extremely intelligent and the older she got, the more devious she was becoming.

Bertram, who was still keeping track of Elizabeth, and corresponding on the case with his friend, Richard Crombie, now believed that each time she got away with murder she became more confident in her ability to elude capture.

In one letter he wrote, *I fear our best chance of catching her was when she murdered the Hamilton family. She was still naïve, and far more likely to make a critical mistake.*

As a professor of criminal psychiatry, Doctor Bertram Killam understood the criminal mind. The more intelligent or educated the killer is, the greater their success at remaining out of prison. When Elizabeth murdered her parents she was just a child and had little knowledge of the true consequences of her actions. Her subsequent release into her grandmother's care had left her feeling vindicated. Had her grandmother still been alive, Bertram believed that Elizabeth's life may have been much different now. He was well aware that her psychotic tendencies were in a category all on their own and now with no one guiding her in the right direction, he worried about what she would do next.

As Scotland Yard continued to suspect that Kenneth Lawson was the 'prostitute killer' another young girl's body was spotted only a few feet from where he dumped his last victim. Officers assigned to keep a close eye on Lawson admitted to falling asleep on at least one occasion. Everything about this girl's murder pointed to him. She had been strangled, her clothes had been removed and she had been dumped like garbage on the banks of the Thames.

Newspapers began warning prostitutes about the murders, urging them to stay off the streets until the killer was behind bars. Regrettably, most of the girls working the streets didn't have that option: they lived a life of poverty and had offspring to feed and house.

Disturbingly, because the police could not build a solid case, Kenneth's high-priced lawyer would make sure that he remained a free man. Kenneth felt that he was invincible and up until this time in his life, he was a bachelor, with dozens of women vying for his attention, and he could be seen in the city enjoying his freedom with a new woman on his arm practically every night of the week.

Kenneth Lawson just didn't have a care in the world and as the cold bodies of his victims, some as young as fourteen, lay in mortuaries, he enjoyed his life of affluence. An arrogant, egotistical man, who flaunted his wealth by mocking police and personally making a large donation to Scotland Yard's sex crime division, he was detested by every officer that worked there.

Although Kenneth cared little for what they thought about him, he did care that his own family had begun to question his innocence. Everyone knew he enjoyed the company of prostitutes and now they were beginning to wonder if it was possible that he was capable of these despicable acts.

By mid-March, there had been no further prostitute murders reported. The last time Lawson had been seen near the prostitutes was 19 February when a police constable reported that he had been trolling for a girl but was scared off when he saw the officer standing nearby.

The police had lost track of their suspect on the night of 22 February. Kenneth Lawson was last seen in front of a theatre near Covent Garden, getting into a carriage with an attractive redhead. No one had seen him since, though his family had not reported him missing.

6

It wasn't unusual for Mr Lawson to be gone for several weeks on end, as he often travelled all over England to conduct business. His maid, Lucy, who had a key to his home, only became concerned when he had neglected to pay her wages on 28 February. Believing he might have gone out of town, she checked his office and found that his briefcase was still there. This is when she reported that he was missing, because she knew he never travelled without it.

During her interview with the police, she said, 'The last time he was home was on the evening of 22 February because on the morning of the twenty-third I came in to begin my daily cleaning and found three full glasses of sherry on the fireplace mantel. They were not there the day before. I spilled some of the sherry on his Persian rug when I removed the glasses and knew if I didn't clean that up straight away that I would get in trouble.'

The police weren't too bothered by Kenneth Lawson's disappearance and this report sat on Detective Inspector Bradley's desk at Scotland Yard for several weeks before it was looked at again. On the evening of 19 March, a boy walking his dog along the Thames came across the nude body of a man lying face down in the river. Although the boy didn't get too close, he could clearly see that a scarf was wrapped around the neck.

The body would later be identified as that of Kenneth Lawson.

An autopsy revealed he died from strangulation, probably with the woman's silk scarf found with the body. There were no other signs of trauma and the police believed he had been murdered, to avenge the deaths of the prostitutes he had killed. A police sketch of the woman last seen with Mr Lawson was distributed throughout London but no one came forward to identify her.

Doctor Killam read a report from the Metropolitan Police about the sherry left in Lawson's home on that same night. The sherry reminded him of the scene at the Hamilton's house in Briarwood. This murder was unlike the ones Elizabeth Riley had committed previously, but the doctor felt that she could have been the red-headed woman seen with Lawson earlier on the evening of 22 February.

It was regrettable, he thought, that the sherry found on Lawson's mantelpiece was never tested for poison nor the glasses for fingerprints. The maid had already disposed of the liquid and washed the glasses by the time she thought to call the police. Nothing inside Mr Lawson's home revealed any further clues regarding his murder, but his involvement in the prostitute murders would soon be brought to light.

A week after his body was discovered, a package addressed to Detective Inspector Bradley at Scotland Yard arrived. Inside the package they found a diary belonging to Kenneth Lawson. It contained a list of the women he had murdered, along with a crude outline of the sexual liaisons he had had with them.

On his last entry, dated 15 February, he wrote, 'How foolish the police have been. Their attempt to discredit my good name has failed, yet the bodies will continue to mount. They simply don't understand that I have done them a great service. The whores spread disease and then produce more bastards that will become a burden to society. I should be hailed as a man of integrity, a hero perhaps, but certainly not the monster they portray.'

There was no return address, but the postal clerk who had received the package described the sender as being a young woman, approximately five feet, three inches with shoulder-length red hair tied back in a silk bow. He also said that she spoke with an upper-class accent, and that she gave him a generous tip.

Although he had described a woman much like Elizabeth Riley, no one connected her to Kenneth Lawson's murder.

A few weeks later, Bertram read about the diary and the description of the young woman who sent it to Scotland Yard. Curious as to whether Richard Crombie felt the same way about the possibility that Elizabeth had committed this crime, he decided to send a letter to his detective friend. He clipped out the article and sent it north with the evening post.

Although Richard did consider Elizabeth for the murder of Kenneth Lawson at first, he wasn't convinced that it was her. This was not her modus operandi. Elizabeth was comfortable behind closed doors and working at her own pace. To commit this murder and dump Mr Lawson's body would bring her too far out of her comfort zone. *Surely,* he thought, *she would not risk*

being seen. And she would have needed help to move the body into a carriage, and then drag it down to the river. No one had ever come forward to reveal Elizabeth's accomplice.

Nevertheless, Bertram was convinced Elizabeth had committed this murder. But he soon began to doubt himself when an arrest was made.

A known prostitute named Agatha Troy fit the description of the woman who dropped off the package at the post office. Agatha had been arrested several times for battery and she had recently bragged about stabbing one of her customers when he refused to pay for her services. She also had an older brother that had been in and out of prison on various assault charges and he could have been her accomplice. A week after her arrest, she was released without charges because the postal clerk failed to positively identify her in an identity parade.

When Richard Crombie heard the news about Miss Troy, he began to wonder if Bertram had been right all along. Although he was no longer working for the police, he still held out the hope that one day Elizabeth Riley would get caught and pay for her crimes. If she did commit this murder, it was very likely that she was now residing in London.

As Bertram and Richard continued to discuss the possibility, he turned to the notes he had written during the Hamilton family murder investigation. It was hard at first for Crombie to believe Elizabeth Riley had committed this crime because the facts just didn't add up. Most criminals follow a pattern and rarely steer away from it.

If Elizabeth did kill Mr Lawson, she was certainly not following a pattern; but then again, as Bertram often said, Elizabeth Riley wasn't a typical psychotic killer. She had her own agenda and until he had a chance to interview her, there was no way to predict what she might do next.

In mid-April, Doctor Killam was commissioned to present a

seminar in London for officers from all over the country about his insight into the mind of the criminally insane.

Bertram personally invited Richard Crombie and asked that he join him afterwards for dinner. Richard was intrigued and confirmed that he would be there. Since retiring, he had become bored and although he had plenty of friends, he rarely ventured out in the evening. A trip to London was just what he needed to spark some life back into his old soul. Despite their age difference, Richard and Bertram had a lot in common and enjoyed one another's company.

Bertram, like Richard, was a humble man, one who never bragged about his accomplishments, or judged others on the clothes that they wore or the amount of money they had in their bank accounts. He was always easy-going and willing to listen to another point of view. His only fault, if you really had to point one out, was his constant whistling.

Bertram was a wonderful public speaker and he had brought an array of slides and a projector to show the audience the kind of individuals he studied. By the time he got on stage the auditorium was full, and people were even standing at the back. Richard had arrived early and was given a seat right in the front row.

When Bertram came on stage and introduced himself, many of the officers were surprised at how youthful he looked. He appeared as though he was a common man who did not wear the attire one would imagine a doctor of his standing wearing, and as he spoke, he also interacted with the audience.

Bertram began by talking about his very first case. It was a teenage boy who had taken an axe and murdered his father. Bertram had been summoned by the defence lawyer to evaluate the boy and determine if he was fit to stand trial.

When Bertram put a photo of the boy up on the projector,

everyone gasped. He was so young and his clothing was covered in his father's blood.

Now Bertram told the audience what they didn't know. Joshua Kindle was just fourteen years old, but he appeared to be much younger. He stood only four feet nine inches and weighed less than eighty pounds.

His mother had died during childbirth and his father had never forgiven him for her death. Joshua had been living in the countryside and never once attended school. His father, Joseph Kindle, had neglected his needs, both physical and mental, since the day he came into the world. Once the boy could express himself, things became much worse for him. Beaten with his father's belt almost daily the child cowered whenever the man was nearby.

Upon examination, the boy had numerous deep wounds to his back and buttocks from the buckle of the belt that was used on him.

On the morning of 3 August 1906, after years of abuse, Joshua had stood over his father, who was passed out from drink, and took an axe to his head, hitting the man sixteen times.

Bertram then put up the crime-scene photos. Some of the audience with weak stomachs got up and went outside for fresh air. The photos were very disturbing. The walls, floor and ceiling were covered in the victim's blood and he had nearly been decapitated.

After leaving this photo up for a few minutes, Bertram then changed it and put back a photo of the boy, this time revealing his injuries. The crowd went silent. Bertram then asked, 'Who among you would hang this boy for this crime?'

Bertram looked out and saw about forty hands in the air. He did not say a word and a few seconds later he put up one last photo. It was the same boy, only completely naked. It showed that he had sustained several unhealed fractures over his lifetime. His ribcage was deformed and his left femur protruded. Several fresh bruises were apparent as well as a deep gash along his abdomen. Bertram than asked again, 'Now tell me, who among you would hang this boy for his crime?'

Not one person raised their hand.

Bertram then continued, 'We never know the whole story until sometimes it's too late and we cannot assume that everything is black and white. This child could have been hanged for his crime, but would he have deserved this drastic punishment, after being abused by someone that should have protected him?'

An officer then shouted out, 'What happened next?'

Bertram smiled and said, 'I recommended some lengthy psychological counselling and I am happy to say that two years after this incident, one of the nurses who had come to know the boy, offered to care for him in her home. The last I heard, he was thriving.' Bertram then added, 'Although the criminally insane patient is often born this way, I believe that some develop these tendencies over time, depending on their environment. Joshua is a perfect example of this. The only way he could stop his father from abusing him any further was to kill him. He had made no attempt to hide after this took place. He was found curled up in the corner of his father's room covered in his blood.'

His next case involved a woman named Connie Atwood. She lived in Manchester and was married to Gerome Atwood, a banker ten years her senior. No one had known much about this woman as she didn't bother with her neighbours.

Bertram said, 'Connie first came to the attention of the police in May 1909 when her neighbour summoned a constable. This neighbour had seen Mrs Atwood burying several packages wrapped in brown paper in a large hole in her garden.' He scanned the audience and saw that a few of them were familiar with the story.

He went on to recount how upon the constable's arrival Connie acted as if the neighbour had lied, insisting she had done no such thing and then refused to let the officer inspect her yard. A few hours later he came back with a detective and two more constables who gained entry to her property.

'And there was indeed a recently filled-in hole at the back of her garden,' Bertram told them. 'Inside, they found the remains of her husband. He had been cut into various pieces then wrapped in brown paper and covered by a few feet of soil.'

Connie was arrested on the spot and during her interview with the police she began acting as if she was confused and had no idea as to why they had arrested her. Bertram read part of the detective's report, in which he said she laughed hysterically when he asked about her husband's dismemberment.

The detective's report also described how Mrs Atwood flirted with a senior officer – which drew a few snickers from some audience members. But they quieted quickly when the report went on to say that when the officer didn't respond she had tossed a cup of hot tea at his face.

'At this point,' said Bertram, 'they brought me in to determine if she was criminally responsible for her husband's death when she committed the act.'

Next, he showed his audience photos of the crime scene and Mr Atwood's remains. Although they were gruesome, many noticed how clean the cuts had been made. 'That took a bit of skill,' said a Met detective sitting in the front row.

'Yes,' said Bertram. 'That's exactly what the medical examiner remarked at the time: skill and patience. Now,' he continued, 'after seeing these photos and the photo of Connie, who among you would sentence this woman to death?'

Everyone, including Richard Crombie, raised their hands. In

this case they were absolutely correct. After interviewing Connie for several hours, Bertram concluded that she fully understood the consequences of her actions. As Connie awaited her fate, detectives looked into her past and found that she had been married twice before and that both of her husbands had disappeared without a trace.

Connie, it seemed, was a prolific killer and had murdered three men. She later confessed that she had murdered Mr Atwood, just to get his £322. Although her death sentence was of no surprise to the officers in the crowd, one man in the back shouted, 'Tell me, doctor, did Connie ever show any remorse for what she had done?' Bertram simply replied, 'No sir, I'm afraid she didn't,' before moving on to his next case.

'My last case,' said Bertram, 'is very complicated. It involved a young mother recently widowed.' He presented a picture of the entire family and said, 'In this photo you see a young couple that appeared to be very happy, all their five children are gathered around them and looking up at their parents, smiling.'

He then read out their names. 'Anne, aged seven, Michael, aged six, Alfie, four, Mary, three and lastly, Sally, age six months. Disturbingly, this photo was taken just eight months before they all died.'

The audience gasped as he showed a picture of the children's bodies. Each one had been smothered while they slept. Their mother, who had tried to kill herself as well, was found in her bed, just hours away from joining her youngsters. She had ingested a full bottle of sleeping powder.

The room went silent as everyone waited for Bertram to explain the circumstances behind this. 'Corrine and Lester O'Brien had been married for eight years and lived a quiet existence. Lester did his best to provide for his growing family, but at times they went without because their modest flat cost him two weeks' wages each month and there was little left over for food. Corrine took in laundry to supplement their income and by all accounts she was a devoted mother and wife.

'Lester worked as a baker, often leaving home at 4am and not returning until late in the evening. His work was exhausting and over time he began to experience terrible shoulder and neck pain. Unable to afford a doctor, Lester ignored his symptoms and continued to work. It was on the morning of 18 November, 1908 that he died of cardiac arrest. Corrine was devastated and after his death she rarely came out of her home. Neighbours did what they could but they, like the O'Briens, were barely making ends meet.'

After a brief pause, Bertram continued. 'Corrine's children were only getting one meal every few days and that was usually bread and cheese.

'Corrine had lost her ability to feed her infant daughter so when she was found, she weighed less than nine pounds. Boiled water and sugar was all that her mother had to give her. Although they were suffering, they were still alive and together.'

'After smothering each child with a pillow, she went to her bed heartbroken and swallowed a large amount of sleeping powder herself. Expecting to die too, she left a note explaining why she had done this and asked God for forgiveness. The next day a neighbour came by to see how they were doing and when she wasn't able to get inside, she summoned a constable. Corrine was alive but barely breathing when she was found but her children were all dead. Although her condition was grave, she managed to make a full recovery. Filled with guilt for what she had done, Corrine would later make a full confession.

'The final blow came when her landlord sent a notice demanding his rent. She was given one week to come up with six pounds and ten shillings or be forced to leave the only home her children had ever known. Corrine begged the landlord for more time, but he refused since she hadn't paid anything in several months. Without anyone to help her, she turned to an orphanage hoping they would take her children until she could find them another place to live. The orphanage only offered to take the infant, but they had no room for the others. Not wanting to separate them, she decided to do the unthinkable, take their lives and leave their fate in God's hands. On the last evening that they spent together, Corrine gave them all warm milk with sleeping powder, then she tucked them into bed. One by one they fell fast asleep.'

Bertram began to whistle as he paced back and forth on the podium. He stopped and peered out into the audience for a moment, before asking, 'Now who among you believe this woman should be hanged for her crimes?'

Only a few raised their hands.

Bertram then asked, 'Is she not a cold-blooded killer?' The audience shouted a resounding 'NO!'

Bertram replied, 'No, she wasn't a cold-blooded killer, she was a young mother and wife who did her best to feed and house her children. Yet a jury of her peers found her guilty of murder! I knew that Corrine would never have done such a thing if she didn't feel desperate and I pleaded with the courts to release her. Surely the torment she felt inside her mind from murdering her children was something she would have to live with for the rest of her days. But instead of listening to me, the courts ruled that she was guilty and sent an innocent woman to the gallows!' The entire room began to erupt in utter disbelief and Richard could see that Bertram still felt guilty for not being able to save her.

Once the room went silent, he concluded his seminar. 'Faced with these three cases, you as officers of the law can see that criminals are not always cut from the same cloth. We as a society must take their circumstances into account. We cannot group each individual into the same category.

'The child that murdered his father would never have done such a thing under other circumstances. The wife who had shown no remorse when she chopped her husband into pieces and tossed him away like rubbish was the only true psychopath out of these three cases. And of course, young Corrine, a woman on the brink of a nervous breakdown, did what she thought would save her children from starvation and misery. She should never have been found guilty.' Bertram scanned the room. You could have heard a pin drop, so entranced was his audience.

'Now remember the next time you come across another murder – and you will – the mind is a fragile thing; it can direct us in ways we would never imagine. But yes, some people are true psychopaths, void of empathy and emotion. It is this type of person that you should fear the most. Not the child that killed his father or the young woman that murdered her own children. A true psychopath will be the most difficult to apprehend.

'Just think about the recent murder of Kenneth Lawson: he had killed six prostitutes before anyone connected him to the murders. Why, you might ask? Think about it, he held an important position in society, lived in a fine house and was highly educated. He dressed in expensive suits, ate at the finest restaurants and had friendships with several very attractive and affluent women. This cold-blooded murderer fooled everyone.

'Now was it his fancy clothes or the company he kept? Yes, this was part of it, but because he felt no remorse for his victims, his overall persona was kept in check. He was void of guilt or empathy and nothing in his day-to-day life ever changed. Mr Lawson just did not appear to be the kind of killer most of us think about. He was handsome, well-groomed and led a life few of us could afford.

'Picture this; Mr Lawson had just left his office and instead of going home, he goes to the poorest area in the city and as he hunts his next victim, is he thinking about her, her life, her family? The answer is no; he is thinking only about his deviant needs. It seems Mr Lawson wasn't aroused by what we would consider to be a normal sexual encounter. No, I believe he was aroused when he strangled these poor girls during intercourse. I never met this man but I would have to conclude that he was a deviant and a true psychopath! One that finds pleasure during an act of violence. Now don't get me wrong, officers, not all murderers are like Mr Lawson, some are simply driven by revenge, jealousy and greed.'

Bertram had now spoken for two hours and fifty-five minutes and after a long pause, he looked out into the audience and said, 'Thank you all for attending, I do hope I have given you some insight into the mysterious human brain.'

Applause broke out, and officers rose to their feet.

Bertram had kept the audience enthralled throughout the evening and Richard now had a new-found respect for this young psychiatrist. He was definitely a man, driven by empathy and compassion.

7

During dinner that night, Richard and Bertram discussed the seminar and when, if ever, Elizabeth Riley might be captured.

Bertram told Richard that her thought process had changed the minute she killed the family in Briarwood. He said, 'Now think of a switch on the back of your head. When Elizabeth murdered her mother and father, she did so without any regard for their lives. Then, for a few years, she remained calm, with no real stress in her life. When her grandmother passed away that unexplainable urge to murder returned and that's around the time she killed the family in Briarwood. I believe Elizabeth absolutely knew what she was doing was wrong in these murders. I think she stages her victims just to amuse herself.'

'And you still think she is likely to kill again?' asked Crombie.

'She must have taken some satisfaction in getting away with the Walkers' murder; just as she had with the Hamilton family. She is probably just having a little break now.' Bertram added, 'Elizabeth, like most psychopaths, can fool many people. They can fit into society and remain law-abiding until the switch goes off in their brain. When that happens to Elizabeth I believe that she will have to satisfy her urge again. Keep in mind, Richard, Elizabeth has a distorted ego and she will thrive on praise and adoration from others. Is it possible that she has an accomplice or someone else that feeds into this need?'

'That line was being pursued when I retired,' Crombie replied. He took a long sip of whisky.

'By the way, Richard,' said Bertram suddenly, 'Did you know the Rileys lived near Kenneth Lawson when Elizabeth was a child?'

'That's a new one on me, Bertram. So there is a connection. She might have killed him, but without the scene staging.'

'It is possible,' said the doctor. 'Though he did have a lot of enemies.'

Richard and Bertram spent the next few hours drinking whisky and talking of other matters.

Prior to leaving they agreed to meet up the following month. Richard liked London, but he wasn't comfortable with crowds, so Bertram suggested he come by his home on his next visit, so he could meet his lovely wife, Anna.

Richard felt he was a better man for knowing Bertram. The doctor had opened his eyes to some things he never understood before. He had always felt that psychiatric ailments were something other people took care of, specifically asylums, doctors and nurses, not something he as a police officer would ever have to concern himself with. Now he was aware that he could have been much more compassionate towards some of the people he had arrested over the years. If only he could turn back the clock, but it was too late. He would have to live with his past decisions, good or bad.

Finding Elizabeth

As spring arrived in London, so did the tourists and the petty crime. Pickpocketings were on the rise and the police who walked the streets had their hands full.

The murders of Mr and Mrs Walker up in Lancashire had not been solved and it seemed as if Elizabeth Riley may have found other ways to amuse herself since there had been no recent murders that could be connected to her.

Tips from the public had dwindled to a trickle and the fear felt directly after Mr and Mrs Walker's bodies had been found was beginning to subside.

All through May and June the police across the British Isles dealt with much less macabre crimes, including daylight robberies, assaults and the occasional domestic issue.

It wasn't until early July that this all changed. On 9 July, Manchester City Police received an urgent call. The unknown woman told the sergeant manning the phone that he needed to go to the Nags Head pub on Ellenwood Lane immediately. When asked why, she said, 'Oh, I think you will know the moment you step inside.' She than hung up before they could get any more details, including her name.

Although the sergeant who took the call initially thought it was a hoax, he sent out one constable to investigate. The Nags Head pub was not in the best area and nuisance calls came into the station from that area day and night. This particular pub had seen the police there several times and most recently to a disturbance relating to a dog fight.

Back in Briarwood, Richard was awoken by a loud knocking at his door in the early hours of 10 July. At the door was a messenger boy, rather out of breath. 'Please sir, Detective Inspector Cross begs your pardon, but would you come to the station right away.'

When Richard asked why, the boy said, 'Two officers from

the Manchester City Police are here and they need to talk to you urgently.'

Crombie was intrigued and wondered what on earth would bring them into Briarwood. As he hurried to ready himself, he hoped that they were there to tell him that they had captured Elizabeth Riley.

He arrived at the police station shortly after 7am and was introduced to PC Anderson and Detective Inspector Myers. Richard and the two officers were then directed into Detective Inspector Cross's office.

Myers was the first to speak and as he looked directly at Richard he said, 'I understand you were in charge of the Hamilton family murder case here in Briarwood.'

Richard replied, 'Yes, but Detective Inspector Cross is now in charge, as I am retired.'

Cross broke in here. 'We've had no further leads, and that case remains unsolved.'

Myers said, 'Mr Crombie, I have the utmost respect for you, sir, and I understand you have recently retired, but I wonder if you could pull yourself away from the life of leisure for a while and assist our officers?'

Of course, he would be working in an unofficial capacity, but still, Richard felt flattered and he had to think about what would happen if he turned the offer down. Unbeknown to his fellow officers, he had been bored out of his mind since leaving the East Riding of Yorkshire Constabulary. Now without any further hesitation, he said, 'At your service, sir.'

On the way to Manchester that morning, Detective Inspector Myers would only say that he needed Richard's professional opinion and any advice he could offer on a crime scene.

This only heightened Richard's curiosity, but he didn't press the officers for any further details.

They would arrive at their destination shortly after 4pm that afternoon and as their carriage pulled up in front of the Nags Head pub, Richard could see that a large crowd of spectators had already gathered there. Outside the front door were two officers who had been assigned to keep the public and reporters out. Nothing had been disturbed inside, but the smell of death and decay filled the stuffy hallway and the minute the officers entered the pub, Richard exclaimed, 'My God, Elizabeth, what have you done?'

The first victim Richard noticed was Rose Keating age forty-one. Myers told him she had just recently become the pub's landlady. She was propped up in a chair that had been placed right in the middle of the room. She wore a black shirt, black trousers and white collar. It was as if Elizabeth was trying to make her look like a priest. A bible glued to her left hand rested on her lap. In her right hand, she was holding a pint of beer up in the air, as if making a toast. Her fingers were glued around the beer mug, which still had some liquid inside and held in the air by a men's tie that was wrapped around her hand and wrist then attached to string which went all the way up to an overhead light. This time, the victim's eyes were glued shut, but makeup applied to her lips and cheeks made her appear as though she was a circus clown. Thread sewn into the corners of her mouth and up to her earlobes forced a smile.

'Like summat out of a nightmare,' remarked the constable who had been guarding the room, when he caught Crombie's grim expression.

Myers murmured to Richard, 'There's no blood; and we think from the decomposition that Mrs Keating was the last to be slain.'

Two other victims, both males, were sitting at a table across from one another. Ted Davies, twenty-nine years of age, was holding four cards in his hand: a pair of black eights and a pair of black aces. His eyes, held open with toothpicks, were directed towards his opponent. A cigar sat in the corner of his mouth and his lips were glued shut around it. The other man, Stan Miles, aged thirty-three, was staged exactly the same way – even down to the hand of cards – with one exception: Elizabeth had removed his tongue and since it wasn't found at the scene of the crime, everyone assumed that she had taken it with her

After the crime scene had been thoroughly searched for further clues, and photographs had been taken of each victim, they were transferred to the coroner's office. At this time, there was no doubt in Richard's mind that Elizabeth Riley had committed these murders. She was the only person capable of this and the only criminal he had ever known that would take the time and effort needed to display her victims.

Manchester City Police had never dealt with anything like this before and they hoped to get some insight into her motives from the now retired detective, Richard Crombie.

Richard still didn't know what drove Elizabeth to do such things and all he could offer was what he had learned from Doctor Killam. He told the officers that they were dealing with a true psychopath and someone that wouldn't stop until she was caught.

Detective Inspector Cross was summoned back to Briarwood the following day to see to a bank robbery. Richard, who was still disappointed in how his investigation into Elizabeth Riley had concluded, decided to call Bertram from the Leeds police headquarters to ask for his advice.

Bertram told Richard that he believed Elizabeth's self-control was deteriorating and that he wouldn't be surprised if she had already moved on to her next victims. Bertram then suggested something that Richard felt might work. He said, 'You should go to the papers and make a formal statement. Now that you are retired you can say whatever you like and I think if you make a statement that gets her attention, she may lose control and possibly make a mistake that will end in her arrest.' This had occurred to Richard before, but he had put it out of his mind, as the chief constable was very strict about what his officers said to the media.

∽

The following day, Richard went to see Detective Inspector Myers. It was easy to see that the detective was feeling overwhelmed. This was way over his head and he had no way of knowing if Elizabeth would strike again in his city. Richard knew that whatever he said wouldn't make much difference: he had been in the detective's shoes, having searched everywhere for Elizabeth, but she was always one step ahead of him.

He then told Myers what Bertram had said and, like Richard, he thought the idea was brilliant. His only concern was exposing the residents of Manchester to the gory details. Richard told Myers that the more they exposed what Elizabeth Riley was capable of, the less likely someone would be taken in by her false charm. Mrs O'Donnell had always said that she was a lovely girl with a ready smile and certainly not capable of murder. If she fooled the wealthy Briarwood residents, it was very likely that she could fool anyone who was unfortunate enough to come in contact with her.

Bertram and Richard knew that she was a master at disguising herself. Her ability to change her accent to fit in wherever she went was just one way Elizabeth could fool a potential victim. If Richard could describe Elizabeth Riley in detail to the public and expose her for what she really was, a cold-blooded killer, he may end up saving someone else's life.

To have the greatest impact, Richard asked Detective Inspector Myers to contact as many newspapers as possible.

Anyone wishing to hear his statement was asked to meet in front of the Nags Head pub on Ellenwood Lane, on 13 July at 8am.

To Richard's surprise, the morning of his press conference brought reporters from far and wide. *The Times*, *The Manchester Guardian, Briarwood Examiner* and Northern Ireland's *Daily Chronicle* were among the many that took over Ellenwood Lane. At the time, Richard wasn't exactly sure what he was going to say, only that he wanted to warn the public and describe Elizabeth Riley in detail, so no one would be fooled by her again.

Richard certainly wasn't used to being in the spotlight and the moment he got out of the police carriage, flashes of light came from every direction as photos of him and Detective Inspector Myers were being taken. This didn't help to ease his mind but he would manage to get his message across.

A few minutes later, Richard stood on the steps to the pub and nervously took out his notes from his pocket. Then he displayed the first drawing ever done of Elizabeth Riley.

After taking a deep breath Richard began. 'First of all, I would like to introduce myself. My name is Richard Crombie and I was the lead officer on the scene at the Hamilton estate, in the town of Briarwood where Elizabeth Riley took the lives of five innocent victims. I must say that at the time most of us assumed that the perpetrator was a man. Once we knew that our main suspect was a woman we began an extensive search. The suspect is a young female named Elizabeth Riley. She was born in Northern Ireland but grew up in London and she is a master of language and can easily change her accent from an Irish lass to that of a Londoner's. She has thick, curly, red hair that she wears up, but I have learned that she often changes the style. Her eyes are blue and she stands a little taller than the average woman. She is educated and can mimic her surroundings with ease. She will dress like the locals, talk like the locals and easily fit into every scenario imaginable. Elizabeth also has the ability to portray herself as a lovely young girl, kind and demure. She may come across as gentle and caring, but make no mistake, she is not to be trusted.'

Richard then passed around the crime-scene photos and the reporters' expressions changed dramatically. He then told the reporters that they would have a chance to photograph them after he had finished speaking.

Once they had looked at the gruesome photos, Richard was ready to continue. But this time he would purposely add some false information. 'Elizabeth Riley may think she will never get caught, but I assure you, she will. During these recent brutal murders, she made several mistakes, including leaving a witness alive. Elizabeth didn't realise that someone had been watching her the entire time, someone that will attest to her every move – as well as to her accomplice. Now keep in mind, Elizabeth is a true psychopath with no regard for her victims and she is not capable of empathy and she may strike again without warning. She is pure evil and I will not rest until she is caught and hanged for her crimes!' Richard then took a few more questions from the reporters.

A seasoned reporter from *The Times* asked, 'Do you know who her accomplice might be? Surely it would have taken a great deal of strength to pose these people after death?'

Richard replied, 'Yes, we have now come to that conclusion, considering our eyewitness statement, but we do not have a name at the moment.' He added, 'Elizabeth is the prime suspect and the mastermind behind each one of these murders. We believe that whoever is helping her is probably her lover.' Richard then concluded by reminding the reporters that the police weren't dealing with an average sequential killer and that everyone should be vigilant about reporting information, even if they believe that it is trivial.

It had been an exhausting day and Richard couldn't wait to go back to his hotel and put his feet up. He was fifty-eight years old now and had forgotten what it was like to be up at the crack of dawn. All he could hope for was that something positive would come from this.

The following day, he returned to Briarwood feeling satisfied that he had done everything he could for the Manchester police.

On 21 July a copy of the coroner's report regarding the recent murders at the Nags Head pub on Ellenwood Lane arrived on Detective Inspector Myer's desk. Elizabeth had poisoned each one of her victims and, as stated by Richard Crombie at the crime scene, the pub's owner had been the last to die.

The two men were given high doses of arsenic, but Rose Keating had suffered a dreadful death after receiving hemlock. This poison would have initially caused trembling, then later it would have paralysed her lungs, which would have left her struggling to breathe. It was also possible that her mind remained intact and aware for a few seconds or possibly minutes, before her heart finally stopped beating.

Less than a week after the newspapers published their articles, Detective Inspector Myers called Crombie to inform him that a young girl had come forward with some information that might lead the police straight to Elizabeth.

Her name was Aliza Singleton and her story was somewhat strange, but believable. Now it seemed that Bertram's idea of exposing Elizabeth's crimes to the broader population with a few untruths thrown in could actually lead to her capture.

8

Aliza lived in London with her husband Brent Singleton and on the evening of 18 July they took in a play at the Apollo Theatre in London's West End.

She explained, 'During the interval Brent went outside to enjoy a cigar with some other members of the audience and I went into the ladies' to powder my nose. This is where I saw Elizabeth Riley.' When asked how she could be sure, she replied, 'At first, I wasn't because her hair was not as it appeared in the papers, but her face did resemble the photo I saw. She seemed like such a delicate creature that I couldn't imagine that this lovely woman, wearing a beautiful red gown and standing just a few feet away from me, could have possibly done what the newspapers were saying. A few minutes later when we were adjusting our makeup, she suddenly turned towards me and asked my name.'

Aliza's eyes filled with tears as she was overcome by the memory of her brush with such a dangerous woman. Myers waited for Aliza to compose herself before urging her to continue.

Aliza went on, 'At this time, I was very nervous but I tried my best to act perfectly calm and I reached out my hand and said, "It's Aliza". She then introduced herself as Elizabeth and asked if I would like to join her and her husband for a drink at the Star Light Room after the play. I calmly declined, stating that I had to get home to relieve the babysitter. Elizabeth then left the powder room and I composed myself before returning to my seat. As I nervously waited for my husband to get back, I could see Elizabeth watching me. When she whispered something to her husband and they turned in my direction, I got up and went straight out to the front of the building to retrieve my husband.'

Detective Myers than asked, 'Did you get a good look at Elizabeth's... husband?'

Aliza replied, 'No, not really but I could see that he had dark, wavy hair, possibly black, and thick sideburns. I couldn't see the colour of his eyes, or the detail of his features, but I could see that he was at least six inches taller than his wife.' When asked if she heard him speak, she said, 'No, I'm afraid not. You know, at first I didn't believe that a woman wanted for these gruesome murders would be so bold as to enter a crowded theatre only a few days after the newspapers printed those dreadful stories, but once I discussed this with my husband, he encouraged me to come in because it was my duty to inform the police.'

Aliza had been very helpful and to be on the safe side, an officer was assigned to keep an eye on her home for the next few days.

Richard Crombie was not surprised to hear that Elizabeth wasn't in hiding. Bertram had said many times before that she was extremely confident and that she probably believed that she would never be apprehended. Disturbingly, nothing about Elizabeth could surprise Richard anymore. It was obvious to him and Bertram that Elizabeth was toying with the police and now he believed that the anonymous phone call to the police in Manchester had come from her.

The day after Aliza came into the station the police looked at the attendance records for the theatre. Where people had bought tickets in advance and had them posted, the theatre held records of their names and addresses. There were 124 names relating to the performance that night; but only one that stood out: a man by the name of Mr Charles Riley had purchased two tickets, three days in advance. The address he had given led only to a post office box, which was attached to a false identity.

The officers who had searched tirelessly for Elizabeth were now confident that an arrest was near and now they believed that the man seen with her that evening was her accomplice.

Elizabeth could no longer travel freely as photos and detailed descriptions of her were in every corner of the country. The resolve to find her had reached new heights and no stone was left unturned. Anyone vaguely similar to Elizabeth was brought into the nearest police station for questioning. The local newspapers also got involved and republished the articles written after Richard Crombie had held a news conference in front of the Manchester crime scene.

In early August, Richard met Bertram in London to celebrate Elizabeth Riley's impending arrest and also to tell him that he would be moving to the South of France. The detective had spent many wonderful holidays there with his retired wife and they had talked about living there in the future. He had never given up on the dream.

Bertram was thrilled with this news and promised Richard that he would join him in the autumn for a brief visit. Both men were beginning new adventures as Bertram had been offered a substantial amount of money to co-write a research paper.

As they celebrated their new adventures, they drank a substantial amount of whisky and by the time they left the restaurant that night, they were inebriated and singing out of tune, at the top of their lungs. It had been a wonderful evening, but it would be the last time the two men would ever see each other.

Richard returned to Briarwood the following day to arrange the sale of his home. It would be bittersweet, but he knew if he didn't make this change now, he never would.

In the meantime, Bertram was preparing for another busy academic year and he had also been asked to do another seminar for the Metropolitan Police. As the two men went about their separate lives, The Met was being bombarded with calls from a worried public.

Every single call had to be looked into but none resulted in a significant lead, until the owner of the Peach Tree Café on Oxford Street came to a police station. Mrs Katie Townsend had contacted the police to say that Elizabeth Riley had been in her establishment earlier that day.

'I'm absolutely certain I served her this very morning,' said Mrs Townsend. She described the woman as being five feet four or five inches tall, with long, wavy, red hair tied back in a ribbon. She wore a white silk dress with a matching handbag and shoes, but did not wear a hat. Katie said, 'I was very busy when she came in and ordered a tea and a slice of peach pie. I wouldn't have really noticed her, except for the way she was dressed and how she had carefully folded her napkin after I placed her order on the table. This is when I looked directly at her and I could see her cold blue eyes staring back at me, like they were piercing my very soul.'

Katie's story seemed believable and two officers were quickly dispatched to her café, but it was too late: the woman that might be Elizabeth Riley was nowhere to be found. The Peach Tree Café was just down the road from where Elizabeth's grandmother once lived and it was possible that their suspect was living nearby. Knowing this, the Metropolitan Police Commissioner agreed that the detectives should enlist the help of an undercover officer. Detective Sergeant Ryan Gomes would be placed inside the café in the hope that Elizabeth would return.

This would begin the following day and Katie was informed that he would be there when the café opened in the morning and remain there until they closed each afternoon. Although Katie Townsend was apprehensive, Detective Sergeant Gomes assured her that she would be in safe hands. 'Madam, if the lady in question does come in, act normally. You just go ahead and serve her as you would serve any other customer.'

'So I'm to act natural,' said Katie nervously. 'I'll do my best.'

Over the next week Elizabeth remained at large, but the undercover officer assigned to this case held onto the hope that she would show up again. From morning to afternoon, he sat in the café reading his newspaper and sipping tea. Gomes was used to the boredom of undercover work and he was quite good at his job, fitting into whatever circumstance he was faced with. No one, except the owner, had any idea that he was a detective. Dressed in plain street clothes, he sat in the corner of the small café, chatting with the regulars. They all knew him by his first name, Ryan. He spun them a story about returning to London to be with his family.

On 17 August, after spending nearly two weeks in the café, Detective Gomes spotted a girl that resembled Elizabeth Riley standing outside. It was pouring with rain and she seemed to be checking her makeup in her pocket mirror. At first, he wasn't certain, but when she turned towards the café entrance, he was sure it was her.

Katie noticed the detective watching the door and as she was bringing a cup of tea to another customer she saw Elizabeth staring back at her.

Katie's hands started to shake but she overcame her anxiety knowing that an officer was nearby. She couldn't let anyone, especially Elizabeth, know she was frightened. She smiled and then apologised, when some of the tea she was carrying spilled on a tablecloth near the customer she was serving. 'I'm all thumbs today. Let me get you a bit of fruit cake to make up for it,' she said.

Without looking back at the doorway, Katie returned to the counter and acted like nothing had happened. She placed a large slice of fruit cake on a plate and just as she was about to serve it, Elizabeth walked inside. She was still standing just in the doorway, so Detective Gomes decided not to make a move. He didn't want to startle her and whispered to Katie as she walked by, 'Just act like she is a customer and tell her to take a seat as you prepare her order.'

Katie, though terrified, did what he said.

Elizabeth was now just a few feet away and the detective held his paper up just enough that he could keep an eye on her without being seen. He waited until she sat down before making any move. After Katie took her order, detective Gomes went up to the counter and asked for another tea. He whispered, 'Now go outside and tell the messenger boy waiting by the lamp post to run to the station and get backup. He's to ask them to send two officers and the wagon to this location and tell them to stay outside the front door.' He winked in a way that was meant to be reassuring.

Katie gave the officer his tea, brought Elizabeth her beverage and then popped out of the door to find the messenger boy. She came back a few minutes later and noisily remarked that she had already asked 'that youth' several times not to loiter outside her café, indicating that she had passed on the message.

Gomes nodded in response and muttered something about young layabouts. He then glared at the café door, as if daring 'that youth' to return, but really he was watching for his officers, hoping they would arrive before Elizabeth left. He did not want to make any moves until he was certain she couldn't get away.

Elizabeth opened her handbag, checked her makeup then took out a book. She sat sipping her tea and reading, unaware that she was about to be arrested. In less than ten minutes Detective Sergeant Gomes noticed two uniformed officers standing outside the doorway.

He caught Katie Townsend's eye and gestured for her to go into the back room. Katie did what he asked and peered through the crack in the door to see what would happen next.

Gomes didn't rush. He wanted to appear as if he was just getting ready to leave. He got up, remarked to one of the regulars that he had to leave to pick up his mother at the shops then he put on his jacket, folded his paper and calmly walked over to Elizabeth's table.

She looked up and saw him standing there. When he didn't move, she asked assertively, 'Can I help you?'

Detective Gomes said, 'Elizabeth Riley, please stand and turn around.'

Two women enjoying their morning coffee immediately realised what was going on. One forgot her handbag as they hurried out the door, pushing past the two officers who were watching the detective through the window.

Elizabeth became defiant, refusing to do as the officer instructed and said in a loud angry voice 'I am not Elizabeth Riley; my name is Marian Crawford!'

The detective then motioned for the officers to come inside.

The two men stood in front of the door as the detective reached down, took her arm and stood her up before applying handcuffs.

As he led her into a waiting Black Maria, she screamed, 'You are all fools, now unhand me or I will be forced to call my solicitor!' By now a small crowd had gathered and Katie came out of the back room to see Elizabeth glaring back at her.

Now the long, often frustrating search for this killer was over. Elizabeth Riley would finally have to pay for her crimes.

At the station, Elizabeth was taken into a small, windowless room, where she was handcuffed to a chair. She had stopped protesting and was now refusing to talk but she did scream an obscenity when an officer was going through her belongings. He found several hundred pounds, a set of keys, a bag of cosmetics, a pocket mirror and a romance novel.

Detective Sergeant Gomes sat directly across from Elizabeth. He could see she was uncomfortable as the temperature in the room was very high and sweat rolled down her cheeks. For the first hour she refused to respond to any of his questions and just stared at him as he sat sipping a cool glass of lemonade. He could see she wanted a drink but when he offered her one, she just stared straight ahead.

Two hours later the only thing she said was, 'Send for my solicitor.'

Detective Gomes made the necessary arrangements and within the hour a Mr Irving Cohan was walking up the station steps. He had represented Elizabeth when she was charged with murdering her parents.

The detective told the duty sergeant to take his time admitting the solicitor. Meanwhile, he watched Elizabeth through the tiny window at the top of the door to the interview room as she struggled to remove the handcuffs.

Half an hour later he returned, this time bringing her a cool beverage. When he set it in front of her, she smiled sweetly, then violently knocked it off the table.

Detective Gomes didn't react. He just sat staring back at her.

When she continued to refuse to answer his questions, he transferred her into a holding cell in the basement. It was dark and dingy, surely not a place where Elizabeth would feel comfortable. As the steel door shut behind her, he heard her scream, 'Bastard!'

It didn't take long before word of Elizabeth Riley's arrest spread throughout the country. Every paper in London ran her story on the front page. Manchester City Police and East Riding of Yorkshire Constabulary, as well as the Royal Irish Constabulary were informed of the arrest.

It was the news everyone had prayed for and Detective Inspector Myers was ecstatic and immediately sent a telegram to Richard Crombie to let him know. He and Bertram Killam had been instrumental in capturing Elizabeth and Myers wanted to thank him again for his hard work.

But the telegram was returned unread and Myers now wondered if something was wrong.

A little later that same day, he called Bertram at his office in the university to let him know that Elizabeth had been captured and to see if he had any idea where Crombie might be.

Bertram was thrilled to hear that Elizabeth Riley had been arrested and he congratulated the detective on his persistence.

'By the way, doctor,' said Myers, 'I'd like to let Mr Crombie know, and thank him personally. But I can't get hold of him. Do you have any idea where I might find him?'

'Ah, he's moving to the South of France. He might even be on his way there now.'

'The South of France? Lucky beggar,' said the detective, enviously thinking of his own retirement, far in the future. 'Well, as soon as you hear from him, would you send me his address, please.'

∽

Over the next few days officers from Manchester and Briarwood came into London hoping to interview the suspect. Although Elizabeth had spoken to her lawyer, she refused to speak to anyone else.

Mr Cohan told Myers that he had advised Elizabeth on the consequences of remaining silent. 'I have urged my client to speak to the police, if for nothing else but to clear her name. But she says she has not killed anyone.' Mr Cohan did not look entirely convinced by his own words. He had, after all, known Elizabeth Riley from her earliest years, and may have had a better idea than most of what she was capable of.

He believed that the only thing he could do for Elizabeth now was help her to avoid the hangman's noose – but even this would be a difficult task.

As the prosecutor, Len Solomon, prepared his case, he found an overwhelming amount of evidence that would prove to the jury that Elizabeth Riley was guilty of each crime she was being charged with and considering her exceptionally cruel disregard for her victims he also believed he would have no problem securing her punishment: death by hanging.

Mr Cohan's entire defence would be based on her diminished capacity. He would argue that she was not of sound mind when she committed these horrendous acts.

Hearing of this, Mr Solomon called in Doctor Bertram Killam to interview the defendant. The lawyer had attended

Doctor Killam's seminar the previous year and respected his expertise.

Now Doctor Killam would finally come face to face with the woman he often referred to as 'the most prolific psychopathic female sequential killer in history.'

9

It took until mid-September before the jury would be chosen for the most notorious female sequential killer the United Kingdom had ever had the misfortune of knowing. Twelve male jurors ranging in age from twenty-two years right up to seventy were chosen and each one was asked a series of questions regarding what they had heard or read about the accused.

Once the jury was chosen, the judge gave the prosecutor and the defence attorney until 31 October to prepare their cases. After several interviews with Elizabeth, Mr Cohan was nervous about her future. All he could hope for now was that the psychiatrist he brought in to interview his client would sway the jury into believing that Elizabeth wasn't criminally responsible, and should not be sentenced to death. He knew full well that the evidence against his client was damning and that her cold and callous demeanour would only enhance her chances of being found guilty.

Elizabeth, although very cunning, would not be able to convince a jury that she was innocent and he had no intentions of calling her to the stand. Each time he spoke with his client, he begged her to come clean and plead insanity, but Elizabeth adamantly refused. His only option was to wait for the psychiatric report and plead insanity on her behalf.

In the meantime, Bertram prepared for his first interview with Elizabeth Riley. He had interviewed many people in the past that he eventually deemed curable, but he certainly didn't believe she would be one of them.

Elizabeth didn't have the capacity to feel anything for her victims and she was far too organised, as each one of her murders had been executed with precision. The young woman had planned every move in advance, giving herself just enough time to escape. Most deemed not responsible for their actions get caught much sooner as they make mistakes; but Elizabeth was meticulous.

Her only downfall was her ego and her belief that she would never get caught. In a letter to the prosecutor, Len Solomon, Bertram called this true narcissistic behaviour. He continued:

> I've seen many patients displaying the same inflated sense of self-confidence as Elizabeth. This behaviour is often seen in people who believe they are better than others, smarter than others and above all, more important than others. I abhor this trait. It can only be regarded as a flaw in the human psyche. And, in my experience, these people also believe they are above the law.
>
> At first, when I attended the Hamilton case in the East Riding of Yorkshire, I had thought that Elizabeth was a revenge killer, but the subsequent cases made me change my mind. Now I wonder if her motivation can ever be determined.

> Of course, I know it is not my job to determine her guilt or innocence, but through my efforts I intend to give you an in-depth understanding of who the accused really is.

~

As Elizabeth awaited her fate, alone in the dark and damp holding cell, she continued to refuse to speak to anyone but her lawyer.

The psychiatrist Mr Cohan had sent in to interview her left frustrated after two hours of pleading with her to answer some questions. Bertram knew she might do the same thing to him but decided he would not resort to pressuring her. In the meantime, arrangements had been made to transfer Elizabeth Riley into a maximum-security prison. This would take place just before Bertram's first visit.

Although he was rarely nervous when it came to interviewing psychopaths, on the morning of his first visit to Elizabeth Riley, he felt anxious. In his briefcase he carried the photos of the victims in Briarwood, Leeds and Preston, as well as the newspaper articles about the murder of her parents.

Elizabeth was standing by the bars in her cell as Bertram walked past the other inmates. When the guard banged the bars with his baton and ordered her to back away, she laughed, then spat at his face.

Prison Officer Brown was a large man and didn't appreciate her reaction. Once she moved away, he pushed her into a corner of her cell, held his baton to her throat and said, 'Do that again and I will shove a dirty rag into your filthy mouth!' He then walked out and stood at the entrance to her cell.

Elizabeth stared at Bertram for a few minutes, then she

slowly walked around him. He could see that she felt in control and that she was enjoying every minute of her attempt to intimidate him.

Bertram then sat down at a tiny table in the back of her cell and waited for Elizabeth to join him. Determined to have the upper hand, he opened his briefcase and took out the crime-scene photos depicting the victims in the Briarwood murders. The gruesome images of these victims all gathered around their dining room table in different stages of decomposition seemed to get her attention. Elizabeth sat down and drew the photos closer to her. A disturbing smile came across her face as she ran her fingers over each of the victims portrayed in the photos. This is just what the doctor expected. Non-psychopaths would have turned away in disgust, but not Elizabeth: she seemed to be reliving the moment.

When she noticed Bertram was watching her, she pushed the photos towards him, crossed her arms and sat back in her chair. After a few minutes of deafening silence, he asked, 'Why did you murder this family?'

Elizabeth continued to stare at him.

He asked again, 'Why did you murder this family?', making his voice just slightly louder and more aggressive. Still no response. He pushed the photos back towards her and said, 'Did Kathleen's grandmother deserve to die? Did she deserve to suffer in agony and did you enjoy watching this frail, elderly woman try so desperately to remove the pillow from her face as you slowly took her life?' Unable to stir any emotional response, Bertram opened his briefcase and took out the newspaper clipping from the time she had murdered her parents. He had highlighted a section of it and began to read it out loud. 'The coroner reported that Sylvia Riley had suffered terribly. Her stomach lining had developed a gaping hole and the stomach acids spilled into her abdominal cavity and oesophagus, burning the mucosa lining as it bubbled up into her throat.'

This sparked a look in Elizabeth's eyes that could only be described as 'hateful'. She then tried to reach over and snatch the article, but Bertram pulled it back just in time.

He could tell she was irritated as she began tapping her fingers on the table and then she suddenly stood up and said, 'Is that all?'

Bertram leaned back in his chair and lit a cigarette. He then pulled his chair in closer, looked directly in her eyes as she sat back down, and said, 'Do you even care about the pain your other victims went through as the poison ravished their bodies? Did you know that dying from poisoning is one of the most painful ways to leave this world?'

Elizabeth smiled. 'That was the whole point, doctor, otherwise I might have used a less toxic method.'

Chills ran down Bertram's spine. He had interviewed cold-blooded killers before, but never a woman.

She looked for a reaction, but he remained stoic, replying, 'I can understand you wanting your mother to suffer, but isn't it true that after their deaths you told your grandmother you were sorry for killing your father?'

Elizabeth slammed her fists on the table and replied, 'Lies, all lies!'

Bertram tried to remain composed before asking, 'Didn't your father protect you?' Elizabeth began to laugh as if something about his question seemed funny to her.

Bertram smiled and then repeated his question.

This time she lowered her voice, almost to a whisper and replied, 'My father and mother were simply pawns in my game of chess. Why can't you see that?'

Before Bertram could respond, she began laughing hysterically.

Bertram then started whistling, but he didn't respond to her comment. A few minutes later he smiled at Elizabeth and said, 'So, Miss Riley, I understand that you will not admit your guilt to your lawyer – but you will admit it to me. Why is that?'

Elizabeth glared at him, but did not answer the question. Then she laughed and said, 'Guilt? What guilt?'

Since Elizabeth was at least talking to him, Bertram felt he was making some progress and when the guard came in to say their time was up, he insisted on extending the interview. With only a few weeks left until Elizabeth stood trial, he wanted to delve deeper into her past and find out if something had triggered this need to kill, or if she had been born this way.

Up until the age of eleven, Elizabeth had been considered a difficult child, but no one could imagine that she was capable of killing her own parents. It was possible that Elizabeth was born evil and that even if she had had a normal upbringing, she would have followed the exact same path.

Bertram lit another cigarette then asked, 'How do you feel about the possibility of being hanged for your crimes? Does this not frighten you?'

Elizabeth smiled and said, 'Why should I be frightened? I am innocent and I will not die at the hands of a stranger.'

Bertram was surprised by her response; she had admitted to enjoying the suffering she caused to the Briarwood family and her own parents. Why now was she trying to back away from her confession?

After a few minutes of uncomfortable silence, Bertram took out a photo of Kathleen Hamilton. He knew she was a strong woman and one that Elizabeth might relate to. How would she react to seeing this woman in such a vulnerable state. 'So, Elizabeth, are you now saying you didn't kill Kathleen Hamilton? Did you not just tell me a few minutes ago that you used poison because you wanted her to suffer?'

Elizabeth stood up and walked towards Bertram. As she got a little closer, she reached out and tried to touch his hair but before she could, he grabbed her arm firmly, smiled and said, 'I think you should sit down.'

Once she had sat back down, she replied to his question. 'Poison works like a charm and if you want to let someone die in agony you just add a little every day, until they are incapacitated.' She added, 'Do you know that when death is looming, people will do the strangest things?'

Bertram didn't know why she wouldn't answer his question directly but because he wanted her to continue talking, he replied, 'What do you mean exactly?'

Elizabeth laughed again then said, 'Kathleen just wouldn't die and although she knew her time was up, she begged me to summon a doctor. She even offered me money to do so.'

Bertram wrote her words in a notebook then said, 'So you are not denying that you murdered these innocent victims?'

Elizabeth's expression changed again. This time she looked angry and Bertram could see the fine lines on her face tighten as she clenched her jaw. She stood up, leaned over the table and screamed, 'None of them were innocent. Each one was selfish, overbearing and obnoxious and every one of them deserved to die!' A few seconds later she calmed down, smiled and said in a whisper, 'But I didn't kill them.'

Bertram then looked directly in her eyes and said, 'So which is it, Elizabeth? Did you or did you not murder this family?'

Elizabeth took a deep breath, then she put her hands around her face as if to frame it and said, 'Look at me, doctor. Do I have the face of a cold-blooded killer?'

Just then the guard came by and told Bertram that his time was up. Although he wanted to continue, he knew that he had gone well past the two hours allotted for her first interview. Now he would have to wait for another two days to see Elizabeth, as the newly appointed defence psychiatrist was set to visit her the next day.

Elizabeth's last comment was very telling as Bertram now believed that Elizabeth Riley felt invincible. He certainly believed that she was aware of the seriousness of her crimes and just from her expressions he could tell not only that she knew the pain she had inflicted on her victims, but that she enjoyed every minute of it.

The next morning the defence team's psychiatrist interviewed Elizabeth in a room away from her cell. This was to stop the other female inmates from hearing all the sordid details of her crimes. In this tiny room, there was no window, mice droppings littered the floor and graffiti marked the cold grey walls.

When Elizabeth was brought in, she was wearing a simple blue frock, a far cry from the expensive dress she had been wearing on the day of her arrest. All her clothes and personal property had been confiscated and stored when she arrived at the prison. As she walked into the room, she glared at Doctor Shulman, her newly appointed psychiatrist, and then asked, 'Why isn't Doctor Killam here?'

Doctor Shulman didn't respond. Elizabeth had been informed by her own lawyer that he had been hired by her defence team, and would be there that day. Although he was a pleasant man, Elizabeth had already formed a negative opinion about him. She didn't like the way he looked or the clothes he wore. He was much more traditional than Doctor Killam and she also assumed he would be boring.

Doctor Shulman wore a dark suit with a high-collared shirt and his demeanour was more like that of her lawyer than her doctor. Elizabeth didn't even like his spectacles and when she demanded he remove them he refused.

Like Bertram, Doctor Shulman tried to get a response by asking her first about her relationship with her own mother. The psychiatrists believed that something must have happened in childhood to spark this murderous rage.

As she sat directly across from him, he began. 'Elizabeth, can you tell me if you remember ever feeling loved as a child?'

Elizabeth laughed and then replied, 'Why do all psychiatrists believe that criminals are the product of their environment?'

Doctor Shulman wrote a few lines on his notepad before responding. 'Did my question make you feel uncomfortable?'

Elizabeth laughed again then said, 'How about you, doc? Did you ever feel loved as a child, or did your mummy and daddy make you feel weak and impotent?'

The psychiatrist was losing patience, but he tried to stay focused. 'It's not about me, Elizabeth. Remember, I am not the one that has been charged with several counts of murder.'

Elizabeth moved her chair to face the door and tapped her fingers on the dirty wooden table.

Doctor Shulman repeated his question, but this time added, 'How about your father. Did he mistreat you?'

Elizabeth was bored with his questioning and instead of answering she folded her arms on the table and rested her head.

Doctor Shulman persisted. 'If you have any wish to avoid execution, Miss Riley, I suggest you answer my questions. You know I cannot help you if you don't help yourself!'

Now both of them were frustrated, but the psychiatrist was there doing his job and refused to leave without at the very least, getting some insight into the mind of this killer. He only had six more sessions scheduled with Elizabeth and the previous one with her other psychiatrist had been a complete failure.

As Elizabeth kept her head down for the next half hour and showed no interest in the doctor's line of questioning, he soon gave up and asked the guard to open the door.

Doctor Shulman had little to tell her lawyer and could only say that at this point he believed she knew exactly what she was doing when she took the lives of those innocent victims.

This, of course, was not what the lawyer was expecting. His case depended largely on the psychiatrist's testimony. Although he was not allowed to interfere with the process, he began wondering if another psychiatrist may draw the same conclusion. There was only one problem: time was running out.

The prosecution had overwhelming evidence against his client and now even Mrs O'Donnell, the neighbour of the Hamiltons in Briarwood, who originally thought Elizabeth couldn't possibly have been the killer, had changed her mind. She was now named as a witness for the prosecution.

During Elizabeth's incarceration, she was kept away from the other inmates. This was not for her safety, but for theirs. Elizabeth enjoyed being in control and on her first night after she was transferred to HM Prison Holloway, she stole the blanket and mattress off her cellmate's bed and threatened to strangle her if she complained.

The terrified cellmate had sat on the floor the entire night. When the guards found her the next day, they could see what Elizabeth had done and removed her immediately.

Now she had her very own four-by-six cell. Her meals were taken in her cell and she was escorted to and from the lavatory and allowed to bathe once a week, with a male guard standing outside her door at all times. Because of her violent crimes she was watched constantly. Hourly checks were also ordered, but they were rarely done.

Although Elizabeth was isolated from the rest of the population inside the prison, she complained constantly about the noise emanating from the cells above and below her. The guards paid little attention to her complaints. As far as they were concerned, she would be dead in less than a year.

No one liked Elizabeth and she returned the feeling. Although her lawyer had known her since she was a child, he often had a guard present during their interviews. Mr Cohan only took on her case for the payout at the end. Whether he could get her sentence reduced to life or not, he would receive a large fee. During the first few days of her incarceration, two other lawyers came by to offer their services. Elizabeth turned them both down. She trusted Mr Cohan. She believed he would not only keep her alive; he could get the entire case dismissed.

She thought it was just a matter of months before she would be released and she had already planned on murdering each one of the defence witnesses.

Mr Cohan had explained to her right from the beginning that his purpose during this trial was not to proclaim her innocence, but to find a reason to keep her away from the hangman.

Elizabeth had been told up front that the case against her was too strong to sway the jury into believing she didn't commit those murders.

Her lawyer also knew she was guilty; everyone involved in this case knew she was guilty.

Now it was up to a psychiatrist to find that she was not criminally responsible for her actions. This was the only way to save her life.

10

The following day, Bertram could be heard whistling as he came down the dingy hallway that led to the interview room.

As he sat going over his notes from the last time he had spoken to Elizabeth, he recalled her parting question: *'Do I have the face of a cold-blooded killer?'*

Today, he would try to provoke the violent emotions he knew she was keeping hidden from him. Elizabeth had thought she was in control during their last session – but the chain of command would be different today.

Bertram wanted her to know that, despite her outbursts and refusal to admit what she had done, he knew exactly what she was like. Since their last session he had read then reread every answer she had given him. He had also noted her expressions and whether her voice raised or lowered. Bertram was prepared and, unlike Doctor Shulman, he wasn't intimidated by her.

Today, he would concentrate once again on the Hamiltons of Briarwood. They were the first people outside her family to die at her hands and he wanted to know why she had chosen them.

When Elizabeth was brought in, Bertram made sure she could see the photos and newspaper articles that were placed just out of her reach. Bertram hadn't even realised he'd been whistling the entire time until Elizabeth had been placed in her chair by the guard and then she asked, 'Do you have to do that?'

He looked up from his papers. 'Do what?'

'Whistle! Why are you always whistling? It's enough to drive a sane person crazy.' Then she began to laugh.

When he asked why she was laughing, she replied, 'I thought you were the expert. Now you tell me why I was laughing.'

Bertram wasn't in a very good mood. A prisoner he had personally recommended to be released into a psychiatric facility had just murdered one of the nurses there and he was devastated. He truly believed that this man would never kill again and that, with psychiatric counselling, he could be released back into society. This was his first fatal mistake. An error in judgement perhaps, but one that had ended with a young girl dying needlessly. It would haunt him for the rest of his days.

Now sitting face to face with a true psychopath, he knew that Elizabeth's fate would be death by hanging and this outcome would not change. His job was to quash the defence, who he was told would be pleading insanity on her behalf. Bertram had only spent a few hours with Elizabeth, but he had already determined that she knew that what she was doing was wrong.

Elizabeth sat back with her arms folded and tried to release herself from the restraints around her ankles. Her recent outbursts toward the guards had warranted these to keep her from lunging at anyone during the interviews. Now waiting for Bertram to begin, she was becoming increasingly frustrated by her inability to move about freely. She hadn't slept much that night, as the noise from the other inmates echoed throughout the prison. As a woman of means, she was certainly not accustomed to her surroundings.

Bertram began by naming every victim in the Hamilton home. As he read their names out loud he watched to see if Elizabeth's expression would change, but it didn't. He stopped when it came to Eric Hamilton, as he recalled something Richard had said about his weight. He now accepted that Elizabeth Riley had had an accomplice.

Although Mrs O'Donnell had said Elizabeth was a robust girl at the time, he knew it would have been impossible for her to have moved a man of Eric Hamilton's size and then stage him on a chair.

Looking at Elizabeth today, he was absolutely certain that she could never have moved any of her victims without some help. Mr Hamilton's stature alone would have been intimidating for an average man, never mind a woman.

Elizabeth had been described as standing five feet six or seven inches. But now the prison doctor had given her a medical examination, which had included taking her weight and measuring her, Bertram knew that she was five foot, five inches tall. She had delicate hands and little muscle mass. Bertram also knew that she had lost a little weight since she entered prison, but that would not have made much difference.

At this point there was no evidence that anyone but Elizabeth had murdered this family and without even asking the question, he knew she would deny it. It was up to the investigating officers to explore the possibility, but Bertram knew they just wanted to wrap up this case and move on. This didn't sit well with him as he knew there was someone out there that had taken part in the most gruesome murders he had ever had the displeasure of being consulted on.

Elizabeth was getting restless. She had been there for twenty minutes and he had not asked her one question. Instead, he had been sorting through his papers and whistling, his mind racing, as he tried to think of the best way to approach her about a possible accomplice.

A few minutes later, he began by reading an excerpt from a regional newspaper that covered Briarwood. 'Crowds of people had now joined the neighbours in front of the house of horrors on Carlton Lane. Everyone is asking the same question: who committed this horrendous crime and why?' Bertram looked up to see that Elizabeth was smiling. He pushed the crime-scene photo of Eric Hamilton towards her and asked, 'How on earth was a delicate girl like yourself able to move Mr Hamilton into this chair?'

Elizabeth stared at the photo as if she was searching for answers.

Bertram waited patiently for a response. She ran her fingers over the page, once again reliving the moment she had killed this man. He did not show his disgust and asked her again. 'Come on, Elizabeth, you are far too feminine to have done this. Even a man of my size would have had some difficulty.' Bertram thought that Elizabeth might enjoy being complimented, but he was wrong.

Her expression suddenly changed and her smile disappeared. She then abruptly pushed the photo back towards him and said, 'So you think I am incapable of doing this? You sir, are not as clever as you think you are. I may be a woman, but I am capable of doing things that would give you nightmares!'

Bertram then changed his strategy and in a thundering voice asked, 'So you admit that you and you alone murdered Eric Hamilton?'

Elizabeth laughed, but didn't answer his question. She liked to keep him guessing and he knew it.

As he struggled to take back control of the situation, he decided to bring Elizabeth's grandmother, Marian Crawford into the conversation. 'What do you think your grandmother would say if she was sitting here instead of me?'

Elizabeth slammed her fists on the table and screamed, 'Leave her out of this!'

Bertram was startled, but didn't flinch. He had finally got the reaction he had been looking for. 'If not for your grandmother, you, Elizabeth Riley, would have spent a better part of your childhood stuck in an asylum. Do you think that she would have wasted her time and energy on a child like you if she had known what you would become?'

Elizabeth glared at Bertram, hate in her eyes. She screamed for the guard but when he came, Bertram told him to go. Knowing she would not talk unless he changed the subject, he put a photo of Kathleen Hamilton in front of her. This time she pushed it away and refused to look at it. Bertram then asked, 'Did you compare Kathleen to your own mother? Was this the reason you murdered her?'

Elizabeth couldn't help herself and looked down at the grotesque photo and then after a few seconds she replied, 'Why do psychiatrists assume that some traumatic childhood incident was the cause of how one turns out as an adult?'

This was actually an intelligent question, Bertram realised. It was obvious that Elizabeth was well read and had been exposed to a lot of psychiatric counselling when she was a child. Her father had been a surgeon so Bertram was not surprised that she had insight into how the brain functions. Bertram then decided to make her believe she was an equal and replied, 'So you tell me why a relatively normal girl like yourself turns to a life of crime and chaos. Isn't it true, Elizabeth, that you have the means to live out the rest of your days in relative comfort?'

Elizabeth smiled, then said, 'I would mislead you if I denied this fact. And if it was only about me, I might have done things differently. Although that's not to say I would have changed anything.'

This statement was a little confusing, but Bertram quickly wrote down exactly what she said. Was she now saying that someone else was involved?

Before he could respond, Elizabeth asked him a strange question. 'Are you planning to live out your life playing by the rules. You know, I would rather die than spend another minute living a life that everyone else does.' Before he could answer, she added, 'Can you imagine the excitement one feels when you do something so out of character that no one can fathom someone doing such a thing; and you get away with it?' Elizabeth began laughing again, but this time, her laugh seemed forced.

At a loss for words, Bertram just couldn't believe that she was trying to explain away these murders by saying it was her attempt to live an exciting life. He knew that she had no remorse or regret, but was she saying that she made her life more interesting and more exciting by taking the lives of others? Bertram sat back and gathered his thoughts before replying, 'So what you are saying is that you believe murdering these innocent people fulfilled a part of you that was seeking excitement? Couldn't you have gotten the same feeling by taking up a sport or travelling around the world? How on earth can you compare what you did to these people with living a fulfilled life?'

Elizabeth leaned over, getting as close to Bertram as her restraints would allow. She said, 'Each time I stood back and examined my work I felt a surge of euphoria rush through my veins. You, sir, may live a life of ups and downs but you will never experience the power one feels from accomplishing exactly what one sets out to do. Now whenever anyone hears my name, they will know who I am. I will live throughout history and someday another woman just like me will continue my legacy!'

Bertram would leave the prison that day feeling even more confused than he had when he first met Elizabeth Riley. She had a way of manipulating the conversation and regaining control. Although he set out that morning to have the upper hand, he left feeling that he had been the one being interviewed. He felt somewhat relieved that he wouldn't have to see her the following day.

~

Doctor Shulman returned to continue his sessions with Elizabeth the very next day, as planned. He could see the disappointment on her face when she walked into the interview room. She didn't like him and although he tried not to show it, he didn't like her.

He still believed that Elizabeth's behaviour had something to do with her childhood, a trauma perhaps, that she had refused to explore during her time in the psychiatric hospital. So he began his questioning by asking about her mother, Sylvia. 'Now Elizabeth, I want you to shut your eyes and go back to the day that you started adding poison into your mother's food.'

Elizabeth thought this was amusing but played along and shut her eyes.

'What are you thinking as you add that first teaspoon of rat poison? Are you angry with her?'

Elizabeth then burst into laughter, but didn't open her eyes.

'What's so funny, Elizabeth? What's causing you to laugh?'

Elizabeth opened her eyes and leaned towards him. 'You. You, Doctor Shulman, are making me laugh. Do you honestly believe this nonsense?'

Doctor Shulman hid his anger, responding, 'Then tell me

something, Elizabeth, if you could turn back time, would you have still murdered your mother and father?'

Elizabeth smiled before replying, 'Of course. But if I had waited until now, I would have gotten away with it.'

The doctor tried not to show his disgust. 'Why do you think they deserved to die?'

Elizabeth replied matter-of-factly, 'We all have to die someday.'

Doctor Shulman then said, 'But your grandmother lived into her eighties and died of natural causes.'

Elizabeth smiled, sat up straight and said, 'Did she?'

This sent chills up and down the doctor's spine. Was Elizabeth hinting that she may have caused her grandmother's death too? He turned to his notes about Marian Crawford, then remarked, 'Her death was a result of heart failure. Are you now saying you had something to do with this?'

Elizabeth's expression changed, for a moment a look of confusion came over her. After a short pause she loudly replied, 'It was her time and that's all I am going to say about my grandmother, so I suggest you drop the subject!'

Doctor Shulman then went back to her childhood. 'I understand that your mother was a difficult woman, one that took her anger out on you. Why do you think she was like this? Did she realise that you were born evil or was she the villain?'

Elizabeth's smile returned as she replied to his question with a question of her own: 'What do you think? Are you not the professional?' Before he could answer she continued, 'For God's sake, everyone in your profession sounds exactly the same. Now tell me, is it because you read identical textbooks or are you all just idiots who fooled the universities into believing you actually know what you're doing?'

Doctor Shulman wanted to reach over and slap her, but he

refrained and then with a hint of sarcasm he said, 'I have a feeling that your mother knew deep down that her child was disturbed. Is that what you are, Elizabeth? A disturbed psychopath, who should never have been born?' Doctor Shulman wanted to provoke a response, have her slip up and reveal something that no one knew about her. He also believed that Elizabeth's mother may have known what her daughter was capable of, long before she exposed her distorted and often vile personality to her classmates and friends.

Doctor Shulman had asked a question even Bertram hadn't thought about. Was Sylvia aware that her daughter was capable of murder long before anyone else was? Did she witness something that may have been disturbing? Her father did send her off to private schools, but was this for her sake or his?

If Doctor Shulman was correct, it was possible Elizabeth had exhibited some inappropriate behaviour much earlier than when she had murdered her parents.

Elizabeth finally answered his question but before she did, she clapped her hands and said, 'Bravo! You, Doctor Shulman, are not as stupid as I thought you were. But only I know the answer to this conundrum. Yes, my mother may have realised... But then again I could have killed my parents for the reasons the newspapers had reported. A poor, neglected child living with a mother that hated the sight of her. What do you think sounds more plausible? What do you think the readers would rather believe? That I was an evil child from birth, or a neglected child, just doing what I could to survive?'

Doctor Shulman was now finding it difficult to determine whether Elizabeth was a true psychopath with no remorse or compassion, or simply insane and not criminally responsible. He was a man of integrity and although he knew that Mr Cohan wanted his report to say the latter, he now believed that it was more likely that she was sane when she committed these murders. All her statements and the way she reacted to his questions, including her inappropriate laughter, all indicated that Elizabeth knew that what she had done was wrong, but she simply didn't care.

She had even implied that she may have had something to do with her grandmother's death. Elizabeth was so evil and narcissistic that she had never implicated anyone else in her crime spree, but Doctor Shulman now believed that this was because she wanted all the credit.

Doctor Shulman left feeling that he might know the reason Elizabeth killed her parents. Although she had convinced the authorities and her psychiatrists that she was a victim, he now wondered if this young woman had simply grown tired of her mother and father.

He decided it was time to contact Doctor Killam so they could discuss their findings. This was highly unusual, but Bertram agreed to meet with him.

If nothing else, they could share their findings and try to figure out what reasons, if any, that Elizabeth had for taking so many innocent lives. This would have to be done in private and Bertram suggested a little café in East London that was just far enough away from any police station to give them the privacy they would need.

Bertram, as usual, would come wearing casual attire and at first their meeting was a tad awkward. Doctor Shulman was a man who went by the book, whereas Bertram was a man that explored many possibilities before drawing a conclusion. During a discussion regarding Elizabeth's need to be in control, they interrupted each other several times. Doctor Shulman was much more experienced than Doctor Killam and he was also old-fashioned and set in his ways and over the next hour or so he would cite several different documented cases of women deemed criminally insane. None of whom compared to Elizabeth Riley. Bertram, on the other hand, spent most of this time nodding his head in agreement in order to be polite. Although he didn't particularly enjoy Doctor Shulman's company or his rather narrow-minded attitude, he did respect his point of view.

One thing that they agreed on, was that Elizabeth knew exactly what she was doing when she committed the murders. About midway into their conversation, Doctor Shulman told Bertram about Elizabeth's comment regarding the murder of her mother and father.

Bertram wasn't quite sure if these murders were planned or if Elizabeth had woken up one day and decided it was time her parents died. They assumed that she had probably been planning this for a while. Their deaths had little to do with her mother's strict discipline, or the fabricated statements Elizabeth had made to her grandmother and the psychiatrists about her tormented childhood.

When Doctor Shulman mentioned her comment about her grandmother's death, Doctor Killam was shocked. Had Elizabeth fooled him into believing that she loved her grandmother? Had her account of her grief been fabricated? Bertram was rarely fooled by anyone and he couldn't believe that he may have fallen for an act that Elizabeth had put on just for him – but it seems that he had.

The two psychiatrists sat for hours on end that afternoon, going over each of their notes. Neither knew for sure if anything Elizabeth had told them was true.

'She is so skilled at manipulation that I can never be sure if I am getting through to her,' said Bertram.

'I myself find her hard to read,' Shulman replied. 'She is a most frustrating and confusing subject.'

If nothing else, Bertram came away from their secret

meeting armed with some information Elizabeth had not disclosed to him.

With this in mind, he decided to take a closer look into Marian Crawford's death in order to either confirm, or eliminate Elizabeth's insinuation that she may have murdered her grandmother too.

11

Bertram had been so wrapped up in his interviews with Elizabeth that he hadn't thought about Richard Crombie for quite some time. It wasn't until he came across several articles that were published after Richard's press conference that he thought about him again. Richard hadn't sent him his new address or even bothered to send along a postcard from his new life in the South of France. This was worrying, so he decided to call Detective Inspector Cross at East Riding of Yorkshire Constabulary to see if he had heard from him.

A few minutes later he reached the detective and was told that Richard had sold his home and had departed on the SS Brighten on 1 September. He hadn't been in contact since, despite making several promises to stay in touch with his former colleagues once he arrived in France.

This wasn't the news that Bertram had been hoping for and he didn't have the time to look into this further.

'It could be that he's just enjoying his new life in the South of France,' said Cross, who was a private man himself.

Bertram put his concerns about his friend out of his mind

and continued to search through the information he had on Marian Crawford.

One thing that quickly captured his attention was how Mrs Crawford had been found on the afternoon of her death.

A police constable and Mrs Crawford's family doctor had been called to Marian Crawford's home after Elizabeth placed a call stating that her grandmother wasn't breathing. The officer arrived first and could clearly see that Mrs Crawford was dead. His report stated that it looked as if she had been dead for some time. He also noted that the deceased was sitting up in a chair by her parlour window, wearing a black dress and a black veil, which he described as "widow's attire".

The doctor spent less than five minutes examining Mrs Crawford and then called for her to be taken straight to the undertakers. The constable then realised that he thought her death was from natural causes. There was no autopsy and her death was said to be from heart failure.

The way she had been dressed seemed very odd to Bertram since Mrs Crawford had not worn black in several years according to a neighbour who gave a statement to the police. He knew that her husband, Jerald Crawford, had passed away peacefully in his sleep on 8 August 1887, at the age of forty-nine. He had been a rather large man who had a litany of problems, so his premature death was of no surprise to anyone.

There wasn't too much information following Marian Crawford's death, except an announcement of where she had been laid to rest. Bertram had not been able to locate a copy of her will, although Elizabeth, he was told, was her only beneficiary.

That night Bertram fell asleep in his study and was woken up at 4am by thunder crashing. The storm had awakened him from a terrible nightmare and he couldn't get back to sleep. In this particular nightmare, Elizabeth was standing over him holding a bloodied knife and smiling. She was covered in blood and as he looked behind her, he saw his wife Anna begging him to help her, but he couldn't move. Just before the thunder had awoken him, he felt the sting of her knife come across his neck.

He carried the nightmare with him into his working day and as he waited for Elizabeth to be brought from her cell to the interview room he tried to shake off the vision and calm himself down.

Inside the tiny, dark room, he could hear water droplets landing on the concrete floor. The sound was getting on his nerves, but he tried to remain focused. Bertram began whistling to drown out the sound even as water accumulated around his shoes.

Five minutes later he heard Elizabeth screaming profanities at a guard for shoving her. Apparently, he had done this to hurry her along that morning. Elizabeth's need to control every situation made prison life very hard for her.

After the guard secured her to her chair, she reached out and tried to scratch his face, but missed. This caused her chair to tip over and she fell to the wet concrete floor. The guard was still laughing as Bertram reached out and helped her up.

Now as he prepared to ask her a series of questions, she decided to take the lead. 'So, doctor, you never mentioned whether you were married.'

Bertram was a little unnerved by this question, considering the disturbing dream he had the night before. But he remained calm. 'Yes, we've been married for two years.'

Elizabeth smiled. 'Do you have a mistress?'

Bertram had no intention of talking about his private life, so all he said was 'No.'

Elizabeth wasn't ready to let go of this and asked, 'Then tell me, if you were looking for a mistress, would you choose me?'

Bertram didn't respond. Elizabeth then opened two of the buttons on the top of her frock, revealing her rather large breasts and asked, 'Is your wife as beautiful as I am, Bertram?' She then leaned towards him, exposing more of her breasts in the process.

Again, Bertram ignored her question and diverted his gaze to his papers. He did not react to her flirtatious behaviour and instead he pushed toward Elizabeth the notes that the attending police officer had written on the day Marian Crawford had died. Elizabeth glanced down at them for a few seconds then she pushed them back and said, 'You know I can be very accommodating, don't you, Bertram?'

Bertram ignored her again and read out loud the constable's statement: 'When I entered the home of Mrs Marian Crawford, I was immediately overwhelmed by the stench that lingered everywhere. I noticed that it appeared as though the deceased had been dead for some time, but I didn't want to upset her granddaughter, Elizabeth, so I didn't mention this to her.' He skimmed over some details about what the old lady was wearing, and about the calling of the undertaker.

Elizabeth showed no reaction.

Bertram continued. 'Her family doctor had stated that the deceased had died from natural causes, probably heart failure. I then questioned Elizabeth Riley briefly and she told me that she had been in town shopping when her grandmother passed away. Since the doctor determined that the cause of death was natural, I left the estate shortly after Mrs Crawford was transferred to the undertaker.'

Bertram looked up to see that Elizabeth was smiling. She then asked, 'Do you have any children, Bertram or are you planning to have some? You do know that they can come in handy in the future and look after you when you get old and frail, just like I took such good care of my grandmother.' Bertram ignored her question and then leaned back in his chair and lit a cigarette.

The constant drip had finally stopped, but Elizabeth had begun tapping her fingers on the table and this only added to his irritability. Bertram was in no mood for her games and when she didn't react to what he just read, he said, 'Tell me about the day you decided to kill your parents. How were you feeling? Were you angry with them?'

Elizabeth moaned as if to display her boredom. 'Can you not just change the subject for one God-forsaken moment?'

Bertram stared right in her eyes and asked the question again.

Elizabeth replied, 'All right, I will play your game. It was just another day like any other. I was in my room and I was thinking about stealing some money out of my mother's handbag.'

'What did you want to do with the money?'

Elizabeth smiled. 'Buy a new frock, of course.'

'So you went from wanting to go shopping to adding some poison to the food of your parents. Why was that, Elizabeth?'

She moaned again. 'Why do you think it was, Bertram? Is it possible that I might just want to have some fun?'

'So, when was the exact moment that you decided to put the poison into their food?'

Elizabeth replied, 'Oh Bertram, why are you asking the same questions over and over again? Do you think that by rephrasing them you will hear something new?'

Bertram tried a different tack. 'When you purchased the poison, did the chemist ask what you needed it for?'

Elizabeth gave him a look that suggested he had said something funny. 'I'm sure you already know that I stole it from our neighbour.' This was true, but he was hoping she would get confused and change her story.

He pretended to read his notes before responding. 'So yes, I see here you did steal the poison. Was it your intention to make your parents ill or kill them with it?'

Elizabeth boldly and without hesitation said, 'Kill them!'

'So tell me, Elizabeth, when was the first time you took a lover?'

'A girl never tells, but I can assure you that I have had a lot of experience.'

Her reference to 'girl' made Bertram think that she had experienced sexual intercourse at a very young age and he decided it was time to ask a direct question about her father. 'Elizabeth, how often did your father come into your bed?'

A look of disgust came over her face and she reached across the table and tried to slap Bertram, then she said loudly, 'You, sir, have a very dirty mind. My father may have been a lot of things, but he was never a child molester!' She then sat back and angrily said, 'Again, you are so far off course that if you were on a boat you would be lost at sea indefinitely!'

Bertram smiled and said, 'Then enlighten me, Elizabeth. You say that you have had a lot of experiences so am I to assume that you had taken a lover when you were very young?'

'Assume what you want, doctor. Isn't that how this works anyway? You ask the questions, I answer them and then you take titbits from our conversations and draw your own conclusions!'

Bertram was finally getting to Elizabeth and he knew that if this continued, she might reveal something about her accomplice, so he asked, 'And does this disturb you in any way?'

'What do you think? Aren't you the expert?'

Bertram replied, 'Can't you just be honest with me, Elizabeth? You brag about being experienced then refuse to elaborate. Tell me the name of the first boy you were intimate with. Did you love him or was it just a bit of fun? You know, like when you murdered your parents?'

Elizabeth laughed then said, 'So you do have a sense of humour. But if you think that you are going to elicit more information than I have already decided to tell you, let me be clear: you are not. You do know that it is all part of the plan, Bertram? Sometimes you have to do things you don't particularly enjoy, just to get to the prize.'

Bertram was puzzled by her answer and asked, 'And what prize was that, Elizabeth?'

'Oh, I don't know, Bertram, maybe seeing my parents take their last breath, or listening to Kathleen Hamilton beg for her life.' She then leaned towards him and in a whisper she said, 'You must admit that the clever way I displayed the victims at the Nags Head pub, was some of my best work, I really outdid myself that day.'

'So, you're admitting to murdering those people?'

Elizabeth laughed then said, 'Am I?' As usual, she was toying with him and again, she had taken back control. Although she had no trouble admitting to killing her parents, she just wouldn't come out and admit to murdering the others. This wouldn't change the outcome of her trial as the evidence against her was irrefutable. Still, Bertram was puzzled by Elizabeth's nonchalant attitude, she wasn't showing any fear and she continued to insist that she would never hang for her crimes.

Now Bertram asked her a direct question. 'So, Elizabeth, tell me something. Did you have an accomplice or will you be taking all the credit for this murderous rampage?'

'Oh Bertram, you are a sly one. Do you actually believe that there is another person out there like me?'

Bertram replied, 'No, not exactly, but I have seen things over the years that would shock even you. Terrible things that I never knew people were capable of doing to other people.'

Elizabeth asked what things he was referring to and when he didn't reply she said, 'Well, rest assured, my good doctor, there is no one out there as creative as I am.'

It was odd that Elizabeth would take credit for how she displayed her victims but wouldn't come right out and say she had murdered them. Surely even she knew that her time on earth was quickly coming to an end, but Bertram was prepared to go along with her if for no other reason than to complete his report for the prosecution.

He was also aware that she liked to be in control and it was possible that this is one thing that made her feel like she still had some control over her circumstances. As this session ended, Bertram had a pretty good idea of who he was dealing with, but he hoped that the next time he saw Elizabeth she would discuss her grandmother's death. That day, she didn't seem bothered by the constable's report. In fact, her expression did not even change when he read it out loud. Although he wasn't totally convinced that she had killed her grandmother, he could not rule that out because of the manner in which the elderly lady's body had been found.

Doctor Shulman had only two visits left when he met with Elizabeth on 18 October. Although he had not found any reason to raise a plea of not guilty by reasons of insanity, he knew that he would have to at least suggest this to the jury.

On this day he would ask Elizabeth what she felt should be the punishment for her crimes but Elizabeth didn't seem bothered when he said, 'Now how would you feel if you knew that the judge ordered that you be hanged by the neck until you were dead?'

Elizabeth smirked as if he had just asked a stupid question

then replied, 'How would you feel, Doctor Shulman? I am guessing that you wouldn't like that very much.'

The doctor replied, 'It's not me facing these horrendous charges, but if I were, I would want to make peace and ask that God forgive me for what I had done.'

Elizabeth laughed. 'What does God have to do with any of this? He can't help me now. No one can and I imagine that when I do die – and it certainly won't be by someone else's hands – that I will go straight to hell!'

Doctor Shulman replied, 'If you want to save yourself from spending an eternity in hell, I suggest you start praying now.'

Elizabeth thought this was funny but didn't respond. Over the next hour, the doctor tried to find anything in her past that he could use to prove that she was truly insane and unaware of her actions at the time she committed these murders.

But Elizabeth wasn't in the mood to talk about this. Her refusal to discuss her family wasn't going to help her or him.

He knew that it would not be possible to persuade the judge that she was unfit to stand trial. And the jury would never believe that she did not know what she was doing was wrong.

In fact, Elizabeth was making things worse because now she was bragging about how artistic she had been when she staged her victims. Still, when asked directly if she murdered these people, she adamantly denied that she had done anything wrong and that hadn't changed since her arrest.

Doctor Shulman couldn't fathom how a sane person could have murdered someone then taken the time, sometimes several days, to stage such an elaborate scene. Just the thought of the decomposition that would have taken place during this time made him shudder.

Although he knew she was suffering from some sort of psychosis, he kept going back to Bertram's original diagnosis, Elizabeth Riley was a true narcissistic psychopath. With the trial about to begin at the end of the month, Doctor Shulman didn't have the time or energy to delve into Elizabeth's ancestry.

Given time, he could have sorted through her relatives to see if there was someone in her family who could have passed this on to her. He knew that people exhibiting true psychopathic behaviour often inherited this from a family member.

Doctor Shulman was convinced that Elizabeth ticked all the boxes of a true psychopath. Her ability to lie was like that of no one he had ever known; and she held herself in the highest regard. She was also bored easily and needed some form of excitement to stimulate her senses. Yet on the outside, like a true psychopath, she could be charming, giving people the impression that she was completely normal, even kind and caring, as Mrs O'Donnell had first described.

As he ended his session that morning, Doctor Shulman asked, 'I am curious about something. Elizabeth, tell me, how did you deal with the foul smells I know you must have endured during the many hours you spent with your victims after they were dead?'

Elizabeth had been tapping the table and avoiding eye contact with him, but when he asked her this question, it sparked her interest. 'The smell was invigorating, you know like when you pass by a florist and they have fresh roses outside in those large buckets!'

'That's disgusting, you know there is no comparison!'

Elizabeth suddenly began to laugh hysterically and she continued to laugh when the doctor abruptly got up, put his papers in his briefcase and called for the guard.

12

All the way back to his home in London's west side, Doctor Shulman looked deep inside himself for any indication from Elizabeth that would change his diagnosis. Unfortunately, he could not find one.

To disagree with Doctor Killam would only make him look foolish to his peers and although her barrister was pushing for an insanity plea with less than nine days left before her trial, Doctor Shulman was struggling with his conscience.

Bertram had already concluded that Elizabeth Riley knew what she was doing was wrong and, unlike true lunatics, her attacks were not frenzied, excitable or out of control. It was easier for Bertram to prove that she was aware at all times of what she was doing and much harder for Doctor Shulman to disprove his theory. Although both doctors were brilliant psychiatrists, only one stood up for the prosecution and he had much more experience with the criminally insane.

As Doctor Shulman struggled to find a reasonable alternative to his official diagnosis, he knew that Doctor Killam was only two visits away from completing his report. Finding this task to be utterly impossible, he did something that would ruin his standing among the psychiatric community. Now with less than eight days before the trial was to begin, he decided to recuse himself from the entire case. Mr Cohan was devastated; it was far too late to call in another psychiatrist and the judge adamantly refused to grant an extension.

Without Dr Shulman's testimony, Elizabeth Riley would not see her twentieth birthday. Hoping to somehow change the outcome, Mr Cohan met with the prosecutor and suggested another option.

If Mr Cohan could get his client to admit her guilt in front of the judge, would he consider a term of life in prison? This plea deal would only work if the defendant admitted to murdering all the people she was accused of and then ask the court for mercy. This, he explained, would save the families a lot of grief as they would no longer have to relive every gruesome detail of her crimes. The prosecutor didn't make any promises, but did say they would consider this option. All Mr Cohan had to do was convince Elizabeth that this was their only course of action and it could save her life.

Elizabeth had to be restrained the day before his visit, because when she was taken to the lavatory to bathe, she scratched the officer's face until it bled. Mr Cohan wasn't surprised by her actions but he was somewhat shocked to see the numerous bruises on her upper arms and a cut on her upper lip.

Elizabeth was in a foul mood and the minute Mr Cohan suggested the plea deal, she angrily refused. 'You are just like all the rest of them, aren't you? A man with little faith in me and one that still believes that the jury will convict and send me off to meet the hangman!' Elizabeth began to raise her voice and although her lawyer begged her to change her mind, she wouldn't.

Elizabeth was also now insisting she testify. 'What have you done for me, Mr Cohan? I could rot in this place and all you would care about is the money you will receive. So let me be clear, I will testify and if you continue to refuse to put me on the stand, I will be forced to dispense with your services!'

Mr Cohan then asked if she actually believed that she could fool the jurors.

'Do you remember the first time we met?'

Mr Cohan replied, 'Yes, of course I remember.'

Elizabeth smiled. 'You believed every word I said, didn't you?'

Her lawyer didn't know what she was getting at, but played along. 'Yes, Elizabeth, I did believe you. Why do you ask now when it has nothing to do with this case?'

Elizabeth slammed her fist on the table. 'This has everything to do with this case. First I was able to fool my father who, bless his heart, tried to protect me when in fact he needed protecting. And then when all was said and done, I fooled the police, the psychiatrists, my grandmother and you! Now, trust me when I say I can fool the jury!'

Mr Cohan stood up and backed away from Elizabeth. His heart was racing as he thought about the day he took Mrs Crawford to the psychiatric hospital and picked Elizabeth up. He remembered how the elderly lady had put her arms around her granddaughter and told her that no one would ever hurt her again. He remembered Elizabeth's cold stare and wondered if Marian had made the right decision. Elizabeth was just a child then and yet she fooled them all.

Elizabeth watched as Mr Cohan tried to hide his fear and loathing. She truly enjoyed making people feel uncomfortable. 'The thing is, Mr Cohan, I can fool anyone – including the psychiatrists sent in to determine my sanity. Poor Doctor Shulman, he tried and tried to find anything in my past that could explain why I may have committed those murders, but of course, he failed. You see, Mr Cohan, I have many faces. I can be the abused child or the housekeeper that everyone loves. I can be a sweet, innocent young lady dating a lovely young man or the whore that plies her trade on the streets of London. But one thing I will never be is someone standing before a judge in a crowded courtroom expressing sorrow for people I didn't give a toss about! Just put me on the witness stand and I will show you exactly what I am capable of. If I fail then so be it: you'll get paid and that will be that!'

Mr Cohan knew that Elizabeth was cunning, but on the day of her release from the psychiatric facility, he did believe her when she told him that she was truly sorry for what she had done to her mother and father. Now he knew that everything she had said that day had been a lie.

Mr Cohan then asked, 'So, are you telling me that you didn't love your parents. Did you ever love them, Elizabeth? Or had you just been waiting for the right time to take their lives?'

Elizabeth broke into hysterical laughter, making Mr Cohan even more frustrated than he already was and he blurted out, 'Just answer my question!'

Elizabeth looked up at him with a stare that would have frightened the devil himself. 'The days leading up to their death were so invigorating. You see, I put just enough arsenic in their food to cause a little discomfort and then I increased it. I watched as my father tried to figure out why he was feeling so poorly and just before he died he asked if I had done this. But, of course, I denied it and sweetly said, "Oh heavens no, father." Now isn't that genius?'

Mr Cohan couldn't believe what she was saying. How could a child of twelve do such a thing to her own mother and father?

This blatant admittance of guilt was all too much for him. His chest tightened, and he couldn't catch his breath. As he yelled for the guard, Elizabeth sat back with a grin on her face that told him she was thoroughly enjoying his reaction.

Without saying another word to his client, he left the prison. As he stood outside, he tried to light a cigarette, but his hands were shaking so much that he ended up burning himself with the match. Mr Cohan now had to admit that Doctor Shulman was right, Elizabeth was a cold-blooded killer without a conscience.

Instead of going directly back to his office that afternoon, Mr Cohan headed to his club. By the time he got home that night he had consumed so much alcohol that he ended up sleeping on the floor in his parlour. The next morning his head was pounding and he hadn't solved anything.

It was his job to fight for his client, despite how he felt about them. He had once liked Elizabeth, even felt sorry for her, but now it took everything he had just to face her again. If he had known what he knew now, she would have remained in a psychiatric ward of a hospital until she took her last breath.

As the day progressed, Mr Cohan's moral conscience began to get the best of him too. With only a week until the trial was to begin, he returned to the prison to speak to his client once again about having her make a confession in front of the judge. Since he had been good friends with her grandmother, he felt he owed it to Mrs Crawford to at least try and work with Elizabeth, regardless of the way he felt about his client. As he sat awaiting her visit, he worried about her reaction. Would she understand that this was the only way to keep her from hanging or would she continue to deny her involvement and let the jury decide her fate.

Feeling anxious, he asked the guard to stay with him during this time. Thankfully, Elizabeth seemed to be in a good mood that morning and smiled before asking, 'Is there something you forgot to tell me the last time you were here?'

Mr Cohan took a deep breath and said, 'Yes, Elizabeth, there is something, I need you to reconsider making a full confession in front of the judge, do you think you can do that?'

Elizabeth began screaming at Mr Cohan, 'I knew you weren't up for the job, I mean how could you be? All I see is a weak little man standing before me, a man that cannot satisfy his own wife!'

Now far too annoyed to continue this conversation, Cohan abruptly got up and walked out.

A few minutes later Elizabeth was put back in restraints for lashing out at another guard.

The thought of walking away from his client had occurred to him, but of course, he knew that he couldn't. This would all be over soon and despite the outcome that he assumed would happen, he would do his best to defend his client.

With only six days left until the trial began, Mr Cohan was feeling overwhelmed and decided to bring in an assistant after asking and being granted a short extension. He needed someone that could be neutral and not react to Elizabeth's flights of fancy. Aubrie Ogden had been an attorney for longer than Elizabeth had been alive. He had a thick skin and wasn't put off by the rants of a psychotic.

Although the judge didn't want to allow an extension, he ended up agreeing to it and he gave Mr Cohan and Mr Ogden one week to sort through the mounds of evidence against his client. The trial would now begin on 7 November at 9am with no further delays.

Aubrie thought he would only make one visit to the prison in order to introduce himself and get a feel for what he would be dealing with because by now the rumours that were swirling around made him think that he was about to meet a lunatic that would cut his throat sooner than agree to a guilty verdict.

In the meantime, Bertram was scheduled to see Elizabeth twice more before the trial started and he arranged to see her that afternoon, before she met up with her new attorney.

The prison warders reported that she had been very defiant in recent days and Bertram prepared himself for the worst. On this day he would revisit her grandmother's death, but first he would allow Elizabeth to explain, in her own words, why she thought Doctor Shulman was refusing to continue examining her; and why Mr Cohan had felt the need to bring in another lawyer.

To his surprise, Elizabeth could be heard singing a hymn as she was coming down the hall and even Bertram had to admit that she had a beautiful voice.

As he sat back and lit a cigarette she came in smiling, sat down without being told and greeted him. 'Good morning, doctor, isn't it a wonderful day to be alive?'

Bertram knew that this was all an act and replied, 'Yes, I suppose it is, Elizabeth. Now tell me why you are in such a pleasant mood?'

'Oh, I suppose it's because I got rid of some baggage. You have heard about Doctor Shulman, I presume?'

Bertram looked up from his papers to see that her expression had changed: she was now grinning at him in the most bizarre way. 'Yes,' he replied. 'I heard – and it seems that you are happy about this.'

The red-headed prisoner stared into his eyes. 'What do you think, Bertram? I'm sure you have to agree when I tell you that he was a complete idiot who didn't have a clue who he was dealing with.'

'And who might that be, Elizabeth? A murderer like yourself that enjoys toying with everyone around her?'

Elizabeth laughed again then moved herself a little closer to Bertram. 'Have you thought about my proposition? You do know that you won't regret it. And trust me when I say your little wife, Anna will never find out.'

Bertram abruptly moved his chair back. 'There will never be anything between us, Elizabeth. Now, can we get on to why I'm here today or do you want to waste my time with this nonsense?'

Elizabeth frowned and crossed her arms like a child. 'Am I not attractive? Am I not sensual?'

Bertram decided not to answer and to change the subject. 'As I mentioned in our last session, I would like to talk a little more about your grandmother. Now tell me, Elizabeth, why the officer who called to her home on the day she died saw her dressed in widow's garb when her husband, your grandfather, had died years earlier?'

Elizabeth smiled. 'Do you know how lovely one looks dressed in a gorgeous black frock with a matching veil?'

Bertram replied, 'So you did change her clothes before the officer arrived. Did you also take her life? The constable's report also mentions that your granny appeared to have been dead for several days?'

Elizabeth continued to smile. 'You know, I look lovely in black. In fact, I think that's what I was wearing when I was arrested… Or was it my white silk dress? Isn't it funny how things all jumble together when you have time on your hands to think?'

Bertram stayed on the topic and asked her the same question again. 'So tell me why the constable had thought your granny had been dead for much longer than you reported to him and her physician?'

Elizabeth put her head on the table. 'This is boring. Can't we just talk about us, our future?'

'We don't have a future,' Bertram said bluntly. 'You will be put to death and of that I am certain!'

Again, Elizabeth laughed. 'I told you, I will never die by another's hands. Try and concentrate on what's important, so we can work out how to get some privacy.'

As frustrated as he felt, Bertram continued to press Elizabeth for answers concerning her grandmother's death. He knew that it was easy for her to kill her own parents, so why wouldn't she have done the same thing to her grandmother?

But when he put it this way to her, all she would say was, 'You know, Bertram, my granny had lovely blue eyes just like you. Were you also born in Northern Ireland? I hear that there are loads of us with blue eyes there.'

Bertram then changed the topic. He could see that she was becoming obsessive in her belief that there was something between them. 'Have you decided what you will say in your defence at your trial?'

'Of course. I will tell you this: I am much more prepared for this trial than either of those idiots that had been representing me!'

The doctor replied, 'You do realise that I will be there representing the prosecution. How does that make you feel?'

Elizabeth moved towards him again, this time brushing his leg with hers before replying, 'Now, don't you worry, Bertram, I will understand that you are just doing your job.' When he moved her back again, she winked at him before unbuttoning her blouse.

'Do you really understand what this means?'

Elizabeth's demeanour changed again and she responded

coldly. 'God, you can be such a fool at times. Do you really think that I believe you'll be in the courthouse to shout my praises? Of course I don't! Let's talk about you for a while. Is it true that the cop in Briarwood wouldn't have considered a woman as the suspect in those murders and that you were the one who enlightened him?'

He had never told Elizabeth about the role he played in pointing the police to her, and he supposed that she must have read it somewhere. 'Given time, Detective Inspector Crombie would have taken this route.'

Elizabeth smirked as if she wasn't happy with his response. 'So you're telling me that the fat old man I saw standing in front of the pub giving a statement would have figured this out all on his own? Please do not insult my intelligence!'

Bertram sat up straight and looked directly at Elizabeth. 'So, you were there that day? You know, I wasn't sure you would take a chance of being seen.'

Elizabeth broke into such laughter that she had to be given a drink of water. At last she said, 'What kind of a fool do you take me for, Bertram? I mean really, do you think I would simply stand in front of the same pub where I left three of my favourite victims?' Again, she was admitting to the murders, but before he could reply, she added, 'Wasn't I creative that day. I mean who would ever imagine a pub landlady being dressed to represent a clergyman! Isn't that hysterical, Bertram?' After a short pause, she continued. 'Don't you see the irony, Bertram, you do know that a landlady can be just like a priest who hears the confessions of the pathetic patrons that drink so much that they divulge their most intimate secrets. Tell me, Bertram, do you have any secrets you want to share with me?'

Bertram didn't comment and decided to change the subject again and tell Elizabeth about her upcoming transfer. 'Just so you know, Elizabeth, you are being transferred to a holding cell near the court two days before your trial begins.'

Elizabeth replied, 'Yes, one of the guards did mention that.'

Bertram was confused: no one except him and the prosecutor knew about this. There were a lot of people threatening to kill Elizabeth and some had even gone so far as to send letters to Scotland Yard explaining how they would do it. Shrouding her transfer in secrecy was the only way to ensure she would get her day in court.

A few seconds later she changed the subject and asked bluntly, 'So, Bertram, since everyone else gave up on me, why didn't you? Is it because you are attracted to my charms?' Bertram soon forgot about what she had said about being told about her transfer when she added, 'Tell me, Bertram, does your wife satisfy all your needs or is she a prude and afraid to experiment a little?'

By now, Bertram was getting angry. Still, he didn't show his displeasure and tried to change the topic again. 'Is it true, Elizabeth, that after you took the lives of these innocent people you went about your life as if nothing happened?'

Elizabeth didn't answer straight away, appearing to consider the question. At last she smiled and said, 'Let's see... I recall spending some time at the theatre, but the last play I saw bored me so much that I didn't stay to see the end of it. And of course, I did go out to the cafés. Bertram, some of them have the most delicious pastries, but if I had avoided the cafés, we may not be here right now.'

Bertram could see that she was enjoying this and decided to dig a little deeper. 'So, you enjoyed spending evenings out at the theatre. When you went out to see a play, did you go with a young man on your arm?'

Elizabeth looked at him quizzically. 'Come on, Bertram, even you should know that a lady never goes to the theatre alone.' As he was about to comment, she raised her voice and added, 'Do you actually believe I would have any trouble stealing the hearts of many young men? I know you might be trying to convince yourself that you are not interested, but I know deep down that if the circumstances were different that you would happily lie with me!'

Bertram sat back and lit another cigarette, wondering how he was going to take back control of this situation, but Elizabeth wasn't finished. Again, in a loud aggressive voice she asked, 'Tell me, when you go home at night and make love to your wife, do you think about me? Do you picture me lying beneath you?'

Bertram was not going to allow Elizabeth to continue with this line of questioning and when she tried to lean into him again, he got up and called for the guard. Bertram had had enough and he wasn't sure when he left whether he would bother going in to see her on his last scheduled visit. He felt that he had collected enough data to complete his report and keep his sanity in check.

One thing was certain: he would be relieved when Elizabeth Riley was found guilty of her crimes and forced to atone for her sins.

13

That same afternoon, Elizabeth's assistant barrister, Mr Aubrie Ogden, headed to the prison to introduce himself and get a feel for what kind of person he would be representing. At the same time, he intended to lay down some ground rules.

Aubrie Ogden had been in this line of work for years and he rarely sympathised with the people he was assigned to defend. In fact, some would say that his manner with them was rude and abrupt.

As he expected, when he met his client, she was much like the others he had dealt with. Elizabeth immediately tried to convince him that she was not the person that the newspapers were portraying. She enjoyed playing games and pretending to be the victim, but Mr Ogden wasn't falling for any of it. He replied, 'Miss Riley, tell me why I should believe one word that comes out of your mouth? Isn't it true that the only talent you do possess, other than murdering innocent people, is lying?'

Elizabeth stared at Mr Ogden as she tried her best to intimidate him, but he just stared right back, saying, 'So, Miss Riley, once you hang – and I suppose you will – are you going to be remembered as the most notorious female sequential killer or just a crazy psychopath who didn't know the difference between telling the truth and telling lies?'

Elizabeth was angry now and said, 'Are you being paid to represent me or are you just another idiot sent here to waste my time?'

Mr Ogden laughed. 'Why, Miss Riley, do you have something pressing to do this evening? Dinner out with friends, perhaps?' He could tell that she didn't like him.

Her gaze was fixed on his eyes, her mouth slightly curled downward and her teeth clenched. Elizabeth was trying her best not to react to his last comment but after a few minutes of silence, she just couldn't help herself and screamed, 'At least during my time on this earth I enjoyed myself thoroughly, travelled freely, ate in the best restaurants, purchased priceless jewels and I still have enough money available to me to live until an old age without ever having to work a day. Something tells me that you, Mr Ogden, live like a pauper and you will probably have to work until your last breath, just to survive!'

Aubrie looked down at his watch before replying, 'Let's cut to the chase.'

Elizabeth slammed the table with such force that one of the legs snapped in half, but Mr Ogden remained seated and kept eye contact with her.

As he lit his pipe, he asked, 'Have you finished with your tantrum, Miss Riley? Or should I wait for a few more minutes? I thought I was dealing with an adult, but perhaps I was wrong.'

She sat back and folded her arms, clearly not happy with how this was going.

Ogden said, 'Give me one reason to save your life, just one.'

Elizabeth smiled at him and calmly said, 'I have told you already, I am innocent. Isn't that enough? Or are you too stupid to understand what that means?'

Ogden leaned in towards her, his breath on her cheeks, but

she didn't move away. In a low, barely audible voice he said, 'We both know that's not true. Now either tell me something I don't know or prepare yourself for the worst. Now, you silly little girl, answer my question and give me one reason to save your life or the next time you see me will be on the morning of your trial.'

Elizabeth looked him right in the eyes, her face just inches away from his and said, 'I guess you will just have to make something up – but I warn you, I am far more dangerous then you realise and if I were you, I would be watching my back from now on.'

The lawyer stood up and called for the guard but before he left, he turned around and said, 'You know, Miss Riley, I think I will enjoy watching you hang.'

Elizabeth really didn't like Mr Ogden and it seemed that he didn't care. He wasn't there to make friends with this young woman, he was only there to defend her. Elizabeth gave him nothing more than what she had already discussed with Mr Cohan and the officers who had interviewed her. The facts in this case had little room for improvement or negotiation. Mr Ogden knew that the jury would find her guilty, his only question was whether or not she deserved to die for her crimes.

Although he disliked Elizabeth immensely, he felt that at the very least, he had to try and keep her alive. Elizabeth would be the youngest female in the United Kingdom that might receive such a punishment and this, he believed, just might tug at the judge's heartstrings. Still, Ogden knew this was a long shot, but worth trying.

With very little time left before her trial, Ogden quickly scanned through the police reports. After seeing the result of Elizabeth's handiwork, he knew that if by some miracle she didn't get the death penalty, she would never walk out of prison again.

As he scrutinised the photos of the Briarwood victims, he

wondered how she could have murdered these people simultaneously, staged the corpses and made good on her escape without help. It really didn't seem plausible, yet the police had given up looking for her accomplice. Surely he should be arrested and charged. Whether Elizabeth had planned and orchestrated the entire thing, the person who helped her was still out there, free to live his life, but he was just as guilty. This, Ogden believed, was simply laziness on the part of the investigators who seemed satisfied to have their main suspect, even though they knew full well that Elizabeth wasn't strong enough to position her victims after they were dead.

It was Bertram's final session with Elizabeth and although he had not been sure that he would go back after their last session, he decided to meet his obligation. This time he didn't bring his briefcase, only a small notebook and a pencil. Their last session had ended abruptly when Elizabeth continued to ask about his personal life and he hoped that on this day her mindset would be different.

Elizabeth was much calmer when the guard brought her in that morning. She smiled at the guard and even thanked him. This seemed very unusual considering her disdain for authority and Bertram decided to begin by asking her about this sudden change. 'Elizabeth, I can see you are in a chipper mood this morning. Tell me how you're feeling about court. Are you prepared for what the outcome might be?'

Elizabeth didn't answer, as she seemed more interested in the guard standing outside the door.

So Bertram added, 'You know, this is our last session. Tell me, how are you feeling, do you think you are prepared for what will happen next?'

Elizabeth sat with her arms crossed and refused to respond. It seemed as if she was still angry with him for rejecting her advances.

Bertram decided to take the lead. 'If you won't talk, I will. Although you can continue to deny that you have murdered anyone, you certainly implied it and I have to say you have not convinced me – or anyone else involved in this case – that it wasn't you. In fact, if I were a juror, I would not believe much of what you say. The evidence points in one direction and that is you, Elizabeth Riley.'

Elizabeth continued to stare straight ahead.

Bertram ploughed on. 'My only job was to determine if you were sane when you committed these horrendous acts and I would have to say yes, you were of sound mind. However, I do believe you have a mental defect and I have come to the conclusion that you are a true psychopath and that no amount of treatment will ever cure you. How do you feel about that?'

She said matter-of-factly, 'You may think of yourself as a brilliant psychiatrist, but you have not solved the puzzle. I know that you have determined that I am a psychopath and I probably would agree, but one of the pieces is missing and sooner or later you will figure that out.'

Bertram replied, 'Then is there any piece of information that you can think of that would save your life? Because you will hang for these crimes and there is nothing anyone, including me, can do to save you.'

Elizabeth laughed out loud and looked directly in Bertram's eyes, before saying, 'I told you I'm innocent and I will never let a stranger put a noose around my neck, never!' This was Elizabeth's typical reaction and by now Bertram was tiring of his patient and just wanted the whole ordeal to end. From the first day he met her she had enjoyed toying with him, taking control of their conversations and trying to insult his intelligence with her denials.

At first, she bragged about her macabre talent of staging the deceased then the next minute she denied having any part in it. She would also go to great lengths to disturb him with comments that were certainly concerning and sometimes grotesque. Elizabeth was an intelligent young woman and well aware of what was about to happen in court, but he couldn't get a straight answer from her.

Bertram, like her lawyer's assistant, Aubrie Ogden, believed that she had an accomplice who should share the blame so that the death sentence could be taken off the table, yet Elizabeth continued to deny this was true. Although she knew it might help her case, she insisted on taking all the credit. Her mixed messages got on Bertram's nerves and she knew it.

When Bertram closed his notebook, Elizabeth knew he was about to leave. Her expression suddenly changed from relative calm to disdain and when he stood up, she asked, 'Bertram, are you afraid to die?'

'No, not really. Why do you ask?'

Elizabeth then smiled sweetly and whispered, 'Oh no reason, I was just curious.'

Bertram could feel her gaze piercing the back of his head as he walked out of the room. He couldn't shake the feeling that she was up to something. He also felt uneasy about her last question. Had this been a threat, or was she just toying with him as she had done throughout their sessions?

Bertram went home that night feeling as if Elizabeth may have sent him off with a warning. It wasn't exactly what she said, but how she said it. That night as he lay in bed beside his wife, he decided that he would send her to her mother's home in Devon until this trial was over.

Unable to sleep, Bertram crept out of bed and sat by the

fireplace in the living room. A large Scotch was just enough to take the edge off and he began to relax a little. This would all be over soon.

The next morning after a sleepless night, Bertram reluctantly took his wife, Anna to the railway station. If all went according to plan, Elizabeth Riley would be on death row before the new year and he would be on his way to Devon to bring his wife home.

Later that day as he prepared for his testimony, he took out his checklist and looked over the five traits most often found in those with her particular diagnosis. Elizabeth Riley ticked all the boxes: she was talkative when she wanted to be and rarely stuck for words. She often criticised everyone else around her. She lied constantly and covered her lies by lying again and again. She continuously admired her self-worth. And finally, she had no remorse or empathy for any of her victims, including her own parents.

Bertram called people without empathy 'God's mistakes'. He truly believed that a soul without a conscience didn't deserve to be born into this world. But there was no way to know how a child would turn out until several years later, often when it was too late and they had already harmed someone. His youngest patient was a little boy. He had been just nine when he tried to kill his mother. Thankfully, he wasn't successful, but now he was living out his days in complete isolation inside the notorious Clareville Asylum.

With just two days before the trial, Elizabeth was transferred to the town of Chigwell. This town was chosen because of the proximity to the courthouse and to keep the number of people wanting to attend down to a more manageable amount.

Since her arrest, Elizabeth had received numerous death threats and two marriage proposals from a couple of lunatics looking for their day in the spotlight. Of course, the death threats and the proposals were never shown to Elizabeth, but she was allowed to read two letters that had arrived from a young woman named Cathy Peirce. They had been read by the warden and deemed appropriate. Other than those letters and visits from the prosecuting team as well as the defence, Elizabeth had no contact with the outside world.

Elizabeth arrived in Chigwell just before noon and by all accounts the journey was uneventful. In fact, she spent that time sleeping and had to be awoken when they reached their destination. The Chigwell police station was rather small and had just one holding cell. Since this town had never experienced any violent crime, the two officers assigned there weren't quite ready for a suspect like Elizabeth Riley and she would spend the next few hours making them as uncomfortable as possible.

The constable was newly married and he was shocked when she made advances toward him. As he sat at his desk reading his paper, Elizabeth called him over and said, 'I was never really attracted to a copper, but for you, I might make an exception. What do you think? Are you up for a little fun?'

When the officer didn't respond, Elizabeth broke into hysterical laughter.

The sergeant fared much worse when he brought her over her lunch, saying, 'Back away from the door, Miss.'

Initially, she moved back, but when he opened the door to place the food inside the cell, she rushed him, took the tray right out of his hand and threw it at his head, cutting his right eye and scalding him with hot water.

The sergeant leapt back up to his feet and locked the door, then threatened Elizabeth with further charges if she didn't behave.

Elizabeth laughed again. 'I am facing trial on numerous murder charges. For God's sake, you fool, do you actually believe

I am afraid of your threats?' Neither constable responded to her comments, but by now, they were frustrated with her.

Over the next few hours, Elizabeth called out several times and each time the officers ignored her, her voice became a little louder. It wasn't until much later when Mr Ogden arrived that she finally stopped bothering them. Mr Cohan would arrive the next morning but decided not to speak to Elizabeth until the morning of her trial. Mr Ogden wouldn't stay very long that day, he just wanted to see how his client was doing and to ask her one last time to name her accomplice. Not surprisingly, Elizabeth was not very accommodating and spat in his face the minute he entered her cell.

Aubrie Ogden wasn't pleased by the welcome she gave him and he retaliated by pushing her up against the cell wall and putting his hand over her mouth, saying, 'If you would like, I can call Dr Killam and have him order restraints. Or we can do it my way and you can sit on the cot and listen to what I have to say. The choice is yours!' He then removed his hand and allowed her to move away from him.

Elizabeth sat on her cot then said, 'What the hell do you want, Ogden? Can't you see I'm very busy today?'

Ogden smiled and replied, 'So, you do have a sense of humour, I was beginning to wonder if there was much more to you than just being a cold-blooded killer. By the way, I had the misfortune of seeing what you did to your victims. Let me tell you, it wasn't pleasant.'

This got Elizabeth's attention and she replied, 'So which one was your favourite? I'm tossed between Kathleen Hamilton and Mr and Mrs Walker, but then again, I think my masterpiece may have been the publican in Manchester.'

The lawyer could see how much she was enjoying this and decided it was time to tell her why he was there. 'The consensus is that you had help during this time. Tell me the unlucky man's name so I can give the judge a reason to give us another postponement, otherwise I have nothing and you will end up in a pauper's grave.'

Elizabeth didn't react the way he expected when she said calmly, 'I know you don't think I am capable of doing these things alone, but I assure you I am, in fact, I still have a few surprises just waiting to be discovered, so if I were you, I would take your silly assumptions and go because as of this moment I have finished talking.'

There wasn't any more that Ogden could do. His hands were tied because she continued to deny that she had an accomplice. As he left he gave her one last piece of advice: 'You have one day to change your mind and I suggest you take the rest of this evening to reconsider. But if you don't, I recommend that you write up a will. I would be more than happy to sign and witness it for you.'

To his surprise, Elizabeth just lay down on her cot and turned away from him, but when he mentioned to the officers that they should keep an eye on her, in case she tried to hurt herself, she burst into laughter. This reaction certainly was more like what he expected after reading Doctor Shulman's damning report.

14

Aubrie Ogden really didn't expect his client, Elizabeth Riley to divulge her accomplice's name. But he had hoped that if he reminded her of the consequences of her actions she might realise she would end up leaving prison in a wooden box.

At this time, Elizabeth was either disguising her fear or she really didn't care and no one could say for sure what she was feeling.

The night Elizabeth was seen with a man attending the theatre had been investigated, but nothing ever came of it and once she was arrested, the police abruptly gave up the hunt for him and concentrated their entire investigation on her. This move seemed ridiculous to Ogden. He knew that whoever this accomplice was, he was still very dangerous and could strike on his own, at any time.

Ogden was as ready as could be considering the short time he had been given. He decided to call Doctor Killam to see if he had any suggestions about getting Elizabeth to divulge the name of her accomplice. Like many people involved in law enforcement, he admired the doctor and had the pleasure of attending two of his seminars.

Bertram was more than willing to share his findings, but he was not able to offer much in the way of convincing Elizabeth to give up the name of her accomplice. He ended their conversation by saying, 'Even if she did tell you a name, how would you know if she was telling the truth?'

With this in mind, Ogden spent the rest of the day putting together a defence that he knew would be ripped apart by the prosecution.

After he left the station that afternoon, Elizabeth remained unusually quiet. The officers assigned to watch her spent the rest of the day catching up on paperwork as they waited for the relief officers that were coming at the 10pm shift change.

Back in London, Bertram was going over his notes from his final visit with Elizabeth. As he came across a few brief lines about her mood that morning, he began whistling. Then he read something he had scribbled down quickly: *Elizabeth seems oddly attentive to her guard this morning, even thanking him for bringing her into the interview room.*

It hadn't meant much to him during their session, but now it was bothering him. Bertram poured himself another drink of whisky, as he tried to recall the guard's name. He remembered that he had never seen him before and he wondered if he had been hired recently. He recalled the guard as being taller than him with dark hair, but he couldn't remember much else. There was nothing that stood out – except for Elizabeth's comment – and even when he had asked the guard to open the door and allow him to leave, everything seemed like it was business as usual. Still, something about the way Elizabeth treated him was beginning to bother Bertram more and more. She had never once said thank you to any of the guards there, in fact, she was generally combative and rude to everyone.

As he finished another whisky, he couldn't let go of the feeling that something about his last session with Elizabeth wasn't quite as it seemed. With this in mind, he decided to return to the prison, if for nothing else but to ease his mind.

The officers at the Chigwell police station were right in the middle of their shift change. Detective Sergeant Oliver Reece and Constable Timothy Knight would now keep a watchful eye on Elizabeth Riley. They would be replaced by two officers at 7am the following day.

Reece would spend most of the night catching up on paperwork as Constable Knight would answer any calls that might come in during his shift. Typically, this station was very quiet and neither officer expected anything more than a domestic call, or a drunk and disorderly. Despite Elizabeth being the most dangerous criminal ever held in this particular station, they weren't concerned. She wasn't going anywhere and her cell would remain locked during the entire night.

Bertram had reached the prison rather late and was turned away at the gates and told to come back at 7am the next morning. Despite his protests, he could not convince the guard to allow him inside and he was not able to get names for any of the guards that had worked on the sixth block, where Elizabeth had been held. This was understandable considering the number of inmates at this maximum-security prison. Bertram had no choice but to go home. But he couldn't rest that night, as he couldn't shake the feeling that there was something he had missed during his last visit with Elizabeth.

∽

Back in Chigwell, Elizabeth was amusing herself by interjecting in all the officer's conversations, including those about police business. As they talked about a report that had to be prepared that night, Elizabeth sweetly asked, 'Is there any chance I could have a look at my file? I'd love to see those wonderful photos again.'

When the detective replied, 'Not a chance, Miss Riley. Why don't you go back to sleep and leave us be,' Elizabeth said, 'Don't you tell me that you're not a wee bit curious about my artistic talent. It really does shine through at the Briarwood murder scene. Just take a look at that family. It appears as if they all adore Eric Hamilton, yet in reality, he was despised by everyone that lived there, including his own wife.' Elizabeth laughed at the disgust that came over their faces and added, 'What did you think about how I staged the Walker couple? Did you find it hilarious to see Mr Walker naked from the waist down? I know I did!'

Although the officers were becoming frustrated with her constant chatter, they did their best to remain neutral and not respond. It wasn't until Elizabeth mentioned the detective's wife by name that he became irate and screamed at her to shut her mouth. Neither officer could figure out how she knew, but it was possible that one of the officers during the day had mentioned Mrs Reece's name in passing.

Regrettably, Elizabeth just couldn't control her outbursts and she wasn't ready to give up annoying the officers every way she could. 'Your wife, Mary is such a pretty young woman. I could only imagine how I would stage her. Do you think she would look nice in a black wedding gown, or possibly a white silk nightdress?'

Detective Sergeant Reece flew into a rage, opened Elizabeth's cell door, handcuffed her hands behind her back and forcibly shoved his handkerchief into her mouth before throwing her back on her cot. He then locked her cell and rejoined Constable Knight for a cup of tea.

For the next two hours, Elizabeth sat on her cot glaring at them and as they enjoyed the quiet, she was seething. Thankfully, there were no emergency calls that night but just before 4am, the detective noticed a stranger standing outside the front door of the police station. He assumed it was just a drunkard, until the man banged on the door demanding he unlock it.

At first, the detective refused, but then the stranger showed him who was with him and this changed his mind instantly.

Back in London, Bertram was beating himself up over not taking better notes on his last visit to Elizabeth. If only he had paid more attention to her expressions that day and what specifically she had said a few minutes after the guard had brought her into the room. He did recall that she seemed to be paying a lot of attention to the guard standing outside the bars and that she had been defiant at first and refused to answer his questions.

A few minutes later, he came across another entry in his notes. He had written *solve the puzzle* and recalled her saying something to the effect of him thinking he was a brilliant psychiatrist, but he hadn't solved the puzzle. What puzzle had she been referring to? Was it her co-conspirator or something else?

Unable to sleep, Bertram went back downstairs and put the kettle on. It was almost 4.30am and he was afraid that if he did fall asleep, he wouldn't wake up in time to get to the prison by seven. As he sifted through the mounds of notes he had written during their sessions he paid close attention to what he wrote in brackets beside them and noted the times Elizabeth had laughed inappropriately.

He had also noted her expressions during their conversations. He had written *she stares at me as if she is staring right through me* twenty-eight times. Still, none of this helped him to solve the puzzle she was referring to. Elizabeth was a skilful liar who rarely slipped up, which only made his job much more difficult.

The last thing Bertram recalled her saying that day was when she asked if he was afraid to die. This was unsettling, but he had heard this many times before. Psychopaths were known for not having a social filter and this line of questioning was typical for someone with very little self-restraint. Elizabeth enjoyed having the final word and was unable to resist taking it after their sessions.

At the station, Detective Sergeant Reece backed away, as the stranger entered, holding a knife against his wife's neck. When Constable Knight attempted to pull out his weapon, the stranger made a superficial cut in Mary's neck then demanded the officer drop his gun and kick it towards him. Detective Sergeant Reece was ordered to do the same and without hesitation, he did.

Mary was only wearing her nightdress and shivering terribly, as she pleaded with her husband to save her.

'I will, of course I will,' said Reece, unbuttoning his jacket. 'Please, she's shivering. Let her wear this.'

But the kidnapper ignored the detective's pleas and ordered the officer to unlock the cell door and remove Elizabeth's handcuffs.

Once she was out, he said, 'Right, coppers, get inside and

don't say a word or the lovely Mrs Reece will die and I'm sure that isn't the outcome either one of you would like.'

Once they were secured inside the cell, he handed Elizabeth his knife and a bag of clothing that he had taken from the Reeces' home. Elizabeth smiled at the officers as she dragged Mary by her hair into the back room. By this time, Mary was pleading with Elizabeth to let her go.

Detective Sergeant Reece, who was standing at the bars, yelled, 'Please, I beg you! Don't hurt her. She has nothing to do with any of this. Please take my life and let her go!' Constable Knight offered his life, too, in exchange for Mary's, but Elizabeth just laughed. A few minutes later Mary could be heard screaming, but there was nothing either officer could do for her.

Elizabeth's co-conspirator sat on the officer's desk without expression, staring straight ahead and ignored Mary's plea for help. Whoever this madman was, he didn't seem to have any control over what Elizabeth was doing and he didn't seem to care.

Detective Sergeant Reece continued to beg him to let her go, but the kidnapper just smiled at him and didn't respond.

About fifteen minutes later the room went eerily quiet as Elizabeth came out wearing clothing stolen from the victim. 'I'm ready to go,' was all she said.

The detective screamed, 'What have you done with my wife? Is she all right? Did you hurt her?'

Elizabeth got as close to the cell as she could, fixing the coppers with her gaze. 'Now don't you worry, Detective Sergeant Reece, she will be fine. In fact, I think she looks even better than she did when she came in – but I will let you be the judge.'

A few seconds later, the two left without saying another word.

Detective Sergeant Reece shouted out, 'Mary, are you all right, darling?' but he didn't get a response. As he paced back and forth waiting for the officers to come in at their shift change, he began sobbing and Constable Knight could not console him.

Back in London, Bertram was no further ahead. Nothing in his extensive notes told him anything he didn't already know. He was feeling a bit foolish because it was very likely, as per her usual strange behaviour, that Elizabeth had just been toying with him. It was also possible that she had purposely been friendly towards the guard, expecting the doctor to overthink the entire scenario.

She wouldn't be mistaken in that either, thought Bertram. He had found himself overanalysing patients since the incident in which a man he had assessed as safe had murdered a nurse at the psychiatric hospital where Bertram had recommended he be placed.

Now wasn't the time to overlook anything and just to be on the safe side, at 5.30am, Bertram decided to return to the prison. He wanted to get there for shift change, which occurred at 7am. He hoped to speak to the guard who Elizabeth seemed to be friendly with.

Bertram knew he was quite good at reading people and he hoped that the guard would be willing to meet with him for a few minutes. He also hoped that the guard would be able to reassure him that he had not known Elizabeth before her arrest.

Back at Chigwell Police Station, the mood was dark. Mary Reece had not responded to any of her husband's pleas to answer him. There was still an hour and a half until shift change. For now, all

Detective Sergeant Reece and Constable Knight could do was pray that she was still alive.

Just before 6am they heard her moaning. This came as such a relief to the detective that he fell to his knees and thanked God for answering his prayers. He then called out, 'Are you well, sweetheart? Please tell me you're all right?'

All he could hear was gurgling sounds and he instinctively knew that Elizabeth had cut his wife's throat. Knowing she could die without immediate help, he stood on the cot and broke the glass that surrounded the bars to the tiny window with his fists. This left him with a deep gash to his right wrist.

Once the glass was gone, he started screaming, 'Help, please help, my wife is dying and I can't get to her.' Thankfully, a passer-by heard his screams. A millworker on his way to begin his day's graft rushed inside to see what was going on. After fumbling with the numerous keys hanging on the wall, he finally found the one that unlocked the cell door.

Oliver Reece was the first to rush out, nearly knocking over the millworker as he ran to see his wife. A few seconds later when Constable Knight was calling for backup, Detective Sergeant Reece ran past him carrying his wife who was covered in blood. He did not wait for an ambulance as he gently covered her with his overcoat and put her into a cab and ordered the driver to go straight to the hospital.

15

As Bertram stood outside the prison smoking a cigarette, the guard that Elizabeth had scratched came out to inform him that the person he wanted to talk to hadn't come into work that morning.

The rather friendly guard said, 'Charles Rigley didn't show for work today.' He then handed Bertram a piece of paper, giving him Rigley's address.

According to the guard, Rigley had started working at the prison recently and had only worked there for a couple of weeks. 'He was a bit of a snob, if I'm honest,' the guard elaborated. 'Never joined us for a drink after work.' Luckily, he was also able to give Bertram a complete description of Rigley, saying he was twenty-eight years old and stood five feet, ten inches. He weighed approximately fourteen stone, with a fair complexion, thick black hair with bushy sideburns and he spoke with a Northern Irish accent. He had no visible marks or scars, and the guard added, 'The female inmates certainly liked him.'

Bertram had heard the name Charles before in relation to this case, but he couldn't recall where. In an effort to find Rigley, he headed towards the address he was given, which was in the

West End and it proved to be a surprisingly expensive address for a man on a prison guard's wage.

It took almost two hours to get to Rigley's flat from the prison. It was so difficult to find the address that Bertram wondered if this guard had given the prison officials his correct details. Within a few minutes of arriving, he would discover that no one by the name of Charles Rigley lived there. This news didn't come as a complete surprise, but as Bertram was about to leave, a young woman called out to him. She had overheard his conversation with the owner of the house and wondered why he was asking about Charles. Her name was Cathy Peirce.

Bertram recognised the name instantly: she had written to Elizabeth. But he kept quiet, waiting to see what this woman would say.

Cathy had known Charles and Elizabeth for a number of years. Bertram started to notice that there was something vaguely familiar about her. Although she did resemble Elizabeth, it was very subtle and when he asked if she was related to her in any way, Cathy said, 'Oh, heavens no, but she is like a sister to me.'

Questioning Cathy further, Bertram learnt that they had met when Elizabeth was twelve and Cathy sixteen. Cathy blushed as she recalled the first time she had met Charles. 'He was such a handsome young man and any woman would have been over the moon to have him on her arm.' Bertram noticed how Cathy's movements became somewhat animated. At first he wasn't quite sure how to take her. Although she seemed more than happy to discuss Charles, she also seemed somewhat protective of him. And when she said, rather boldly, 'Charles Rigley and I are lovers. One day we plan to get married!' Bertram was taken aback, because moments later she added, 'Can you imagine a grown man falling in love with a child? It's sinful, that's what it is.'

'Do you mean you were a child when Mr Rigley... fell in love with you?'

'No,' said Cathy. 'I mean her. Elizabeth. He loved her from the day they met.'

'Are you telling me that Elizabeth and Charles were lovers when she was just a child of twelve?'

Cathy turned away from the doctor as if embarrassed by what she was about to relate. 'Yes, that's exactly what I am telling you. But still, I know he'll come back to me: he always does.'

Bertram could see that Cathy felt somewhat inferior to Elizabeth and turned his attention back to her by asking, 'Do you still see Charles?'

Cathy smiled shyly and then replied, 'Yes, as much as he will allow.' A few seconds later, she added, 'But Elizabeth must never find out.'

Bertram wasn't sure what she meant by this; didn't she know that Elizabeth was likely to die for her crimes? This being her future, he replied, 'Surely you are not afraid of Elizabeth now? She will only leave prison in a pine box and she will never be able to hurt anyone else.' Bertram could see that this statement upset her, but he didn't understand why.

He then noticed how Cathy had suddenly stopped talking and diverted her gaze away from him. He was beginning to believe that she knew something more than she was telling, and he wasn't about to leave until he at least tried to find out what it was.

After a few minutes of uncomfortable silence, he began whistling and when he realised what he was doing, he stopped and then suggested they take a short walk down to the teahouse and discuss her relationship with Charles. Talking about Charles seemed to spark her interest again and as they strolled down the road, they noticed neighbours peering out of their windows.

Cathy glanced up at Bertram and immediately took his arm, then said loudly, 'Shall we give the old hags something to talk about?'

Bertram was now curious as to why this seemingly normal young woman would associate with a known murderer and he also wondered if she knew that Charles had been involved. Throughout the conversation, Cathy went from a quiet and withdrawn young woman to a brash, often loud one who seemed at times to have little control of her emotions.

As he discussed Elizabeth's lengthy criminal history, it wasn't long before she confessed to believing that she initially thought that Elizabeth Riley was innocent of these crimes.

When Bertram asked why she would believe such a thing, she replied, 'Charles had come by after the murders in the pub and told me not to pay any attention to the newspaper reports. He said they were trying to blame Elizabeth for these gruesome acts and that none of it was true.' Cathy smiled shyly. 'You have to understand what kind of man Charles is. You know when we met that all the girls idolised him. It was as if whatever he said was the absolute truth. He was like my pastor and no one, including me, ever questioned him. So, you see, I did believe him when he told me she was innocent but then when he disappeared again, I began to hear more dreadful stories about Elizabeth and that's when I started reading all the articles about her, including the ones from Briarwood. I knew then that she had done this after seeing the photos of her victims.'

When Bertram delved a little deeper and asked Cathy why she now believed Elizabeth to be guilty, she startled him by saying, 'Elizabeth seemed to be drawn to the strangest things and when her grandmother died, she invited me and Charles into her home to see her. I was mortified, but Charles took it all with a pinch of salt. When Elizabeth asked him to help her take her granny from her bed, down to the parlour, he did so willingly. Her granny was in her nightdress, but then Elizabeth decided to change her clothes and she asked Charles to fetch the black dress her grandmother had worn to her husband's funeral from her wardrobe. Charles didn't seem to mind and within a few minutes he returned with the items that Elizabeth asked for. By this time, the smell was beginning to make me feel ill, but it didn't seem to bother either of them.'

Cathy paused, as if sickened by the memory and then continued. 'I didn't want to see what her plans were, but Charles decided to stay and he later told me how he helped Elizabeth put her granny's black widow's weeds on her and then he said how Elizabeth laughed when she covered her face with a veil and told him that she thought she looked better in death than she had ever looked in life.'

Cathy also confessed to still being in love with Charles and having taken him to her bed recently. When asked how recently, she looked down at her belly and said, 'I'm not really sure.'

Bertram then glanced down at her stomach and noted the bulge. Cathy, it seemed, was pregnant with Charles' child.

Bertram then asked the question he already knew the answer to: 'So tell me, Cathy, did Charles recently begin a job at the prison?'

Cathy replied without hesitation, 'Oh yes, he started there a few weeks ago, I think he just wanted to be closer to Elizabeth in her time of need.'

Finally, after months of dealing with Elizabeth's misleading and untruthful conversations, Bertram was putting the puzzle pieces together. Cathy still wasn't willing to say that she was absolutely sure that Charles had killed these people, but she did admit that Elizabeth couldn't have done what the detective's reports said she had without some help.

Bertram asked her why she didn't tell the police what she had just told him and she replied matter-of-factly, 'No one ever asked me.' Then she smiled and added, 'Even if they did, I would have lied, because Elizabeth can be very dangerous and I do still love Charles.'

Bertram then asked, 'Are you afraid of Elizabeth?'

Cathy turned away from him again and then replied rather quietly, 'No, not really.'

Bertram left, feeling somewhat anxious about what she had told him. With this overwhelming sense that something was not right, he didn't waste any more time and headed straight to The Met. If all was well, he knew that at the very least, this information would be very useful for the prosecutor. Bertram now had the name of Elizabeth's accomplice, as well as a full description of this man.

Sadly, at this point he still had no idea that she had escaped and had gravely injured an officer's wife.

Back in Chigwell, Mary Reece was undergoing surgery to close the artery that Elizabeth had tried to sever when she cut her throat from ear to ear. Thankfully, Detective Sergeant Oliver Reece had some medical training and had held a cloth to her throat as he transferred his wife to the hospital. This, he was told, had probably saved her life.

Disturbingly, Elizabeth hadn't stopped at Mary's throat and had made several deeper cuts to her face. She had slashed both sides of her mouth from the outer edges to just under her ear lobes.

Mary, if she survived, would have to live with these scars for the rest of her life, but the inner torture she would endure would be much more damaging.

When Bertram arrived at Chigwell, he immediately sensed that the officers were in a hyper-vigilant state. The station was swarming with police from all over England and all were huddled together talking quietly about something that he couldn't quite hear.

It wasn't until he saw Elizabeth's lawyer's, Mr Cohan and Mr Ogden with the prosecutor Len Solomon, that he knew his worst nightmare was about to come true. The two lawyers went into an office and when Bertram went to follow, they shut the door on him.

As he stood there waiting to find out what was going on, he began whistling, not realising that the sound was getting on the police officers' nerves until one piped up, 'Doctor Killam, do you mind, we are trying to concentrate!'

Bertram apologised: sometimes he didn't realise how loud he could be, and to stop this nervous habit, he smoked one cigarette after another, while pacing back and forth.

Twenty minutes later, Ogden came out and told Bertram to follow him. As they walked down the street, Aubrie remained tight-lipped until they finally came to their destination, The Bull's Eye Tavern. Aubrie ordered two large whiskys before telling Bertram what was going on. Bertram was exhausted and hungover from overindulging the night before, but he still managed to get the whisky down his throat.

This is when Aubrie explained everything that had taken place in Chigwell, including how Elizabeth had taken Mary Reece's clothing off and redressed her in the prison frock she was wearing, just before cutting her throat.

This news made Bertram feel sick to his stomach and then his thoughts turned to his own wife. Elizabeth had referred to her several times in their last few sessions and now he was terrified that she would hurt her too. With this weighing heavily on his mind, he left the pub immediately and headed home to pack some clothing.

Shortly after he arrived, his neighbour's son came to his

door. This young lad told Bertram that he had been approached by a man fitting Charles Rigley's description, who then asked that he deliver a letter directly to Doctor Killam on 7 November. The lad didn't mind doing this, as this stranger had generously given him a half crown for his troubles. Although Bertram had drunk more than his fill in the past two days, he poured himself a large whisky before opening the envelope. Inside, he found a letter from Elizabeth, dated 3 November, only two days before she was transferred to Chigwell.

My darling Bertram,
As you must know by now, I have done what everyone including yourself had deemed impossible. Now, I must ask, how does it feel to find out that you failed miserably? Please, darling, don't take this to heart, as I do know you tried.
Still, I did warn you that you should not underestimate my resolve and anyone who believed I would sit back and allow twelve strangers to decide my fate is a fool.
Despite your obvious insecurities and many, many flaws, I did find your commitment to your wife to be quite admirable and, of course, this only made me more attracted to you. Isn't it strange how when I can't get what I want in life, it makes me want it more? This, I believe you referred to at one time, as being selfish, narcissistic behaviour and unbecoming of a young lady, like myself. So, you see, Bertram, I was listening.
That's the funny thing about people like me: we can easily move on to the next adventure, without ever thinking about what we leave behind. If only you had been there to see how well I had planned and executed my escape, but who knows, maybe one day down the road, I can tell you all about it. Now, as you sit and contemplate my next move, which I know you will, remain rest assured that I will always be close by and yet just far enough away to avoid capture.
Until next time my darling,

Elizabeth.

Now even more concerned about his wife, Bertram sent a telegram to Anna who replied by return assuring him that she was in good health. Still not convinced that she was safe, he prepared to go to Devon the following morning. Bertram had had a first-hand look at what Elizabeth was capable of, and he knew that she was still angry with him for ignoring her advances, possibly angry enough to take it out on his wife.

Shortly after Bertram and Ogden parted ways, the lawyer returned to Scotland Yard and gave the commissioner the name and description of Elizabeth's lover and co-conspirator. This news was extremely troubling to the commissioner and he was completely taken aback by his fellow officers who he now called 'negligent and irresponsible individuals, not worthy of the badge they wear'.

He asked Ogden to join him for a press conference in which he would tell the reporters everything he had told him, including the full description of the suspect. During this conference, Ogden would also tell the reporters something he and Bertram had concluded. Although Charles Rigley – who sometimes used the surname Riley – was equally guilty of these murders, he was probably not the one instigating these crimes.

When a reporter asked him to clarify this, the commissioner said, 'Make no mistake, Charles Rigley is a dangerous man, but Elizabeth Riley should be considered even more dangerous. Doctor Killam, a renowned criminal psychiatrist who has worked with this force many times, came to the conclusion that Elizabeth was far more likely to be the one calling all the shots.'

The press was then given a full description of Charles Rigley and told of the last location where the two suspects had been seen.

As Great Britain held its collective breath waiting for

Elizabeth and Charles to be apprehended, Bertram was finding it hard to keep his eyes open, as the train he was on gently rocked back and forth during his trip to Devon. Unfortunately, each time he dozed off, the nightmare of Elizabeth standing over him with a knife covered in blood and his wife begging for help entered his dreams. This horrific scene wouldn't allow him to get a restful sleep and by the time he arrived at his destination, he felt weak and disoriented.

It was not until he lay in his wife's arms later that night that he could finally relax and catch up on some much-needed sleep.

Back in London, every available officer was looking for Elizabeth and Charles. Although the town of Chigwell was under lockdown there had not been one sighting of the suspects since they slipped out of the police station in the early morning hours. Detective Sergeant Reece was not involved in this search as he had not left his wife's side since she came out of surgery. Mary Ann was still on the critical list. She was still alive but the doctors were not making any promises. She had lost a lot of blood and this had caused her blood pressure to plummet and destabilise her further.

It was a worrying time for her husband, Detective Sergeant Oliver Reece, who sat by her bed, still covered in his wife's blood. Pleas by the nursing staff to go home and take a break naturally went unanswered. As long as Mary remained in a critical condition, he was going nowhere.

Two days after arriving in Devon, Bertram received an unexpected letter. There was no postmark and he assumed that someone had hand-delivered it. The front of the envelope was addressed to Bertram Killam c/o 129 Frederick Lane, Appledore, Devon. It had no return address.

Inside the envelope, he found a key and a note with the address and directions to a storage locker in Briarwood. Nothing else was written on this note and there was nothing to indicate what was inside that locker and no one, including Anna's mother, who arose very early, had seen who delivered this. As Bertram held this mysterious key in his hand, rolling it over his fingers, his thoughts of who might have delivered this went straight to Elizabeth Riley.

Bertram's anxiety would grow substantially, after realising Elizabeth had just been a three-inch-thick wooden door away from his family. Knowing that she had found him in Devon made him wonder if there was any place left in England where he could take his family and feel safe.

To ensure that he didn't upset his wife any further, Bertram kept his thoughts to himself. She had already been disrupted by all of this, and deep down, he now blamed himself for ever taking on this case.

16

Bertram made an excuse to go into the village and use the telephone at the post office to make a call to The Met to inform them that he believed Elizabeth had been in Devon earlier that day. Although his call should have been made much earlier, they told him that he had been the second person to call informing them that Elizabeth might have passed through Devon.

A farmer had noticed a man and a woman fitting the suspects' descriptions go past his yard in a covered carriage. The sighting had been at 5.30 that morning and he said it appeared as though they were going west toward the town of Dittisham.

To know they were heading away from Devon was a relief to Bertram, but still, he had to wonder why she had come there in the first place. One thing was certain, Elizabeth had to be in control and it was possible that she had shown up at his in-laws just to prove that point.

Back in Chigwell, Mary Reece's condition remained unstable as she fought off an infection. This had developed in her cheek after she awoke for a short time and in her confusion tried to pull out her sutures. This opened the wounds and as soon as the nurses noticed she was rushed back into surgery.

Detective Sergeant Oliver Reece had now been at the hospital for three days and was still refusing to leave his wife's side. His suit began to smell from the blood and the hospital staff had to insist that he go home to bathe and change his clothes. He was escorted home by a colleague but returned within the hour. By this time exhaustion had taken over and when his wife got back from surgery, he had fallen asleep in the chair beside her bed. He was still asleep when she took her last breath.

Back in London, everyone was on edge and pressure from the public and government officials to solve this case was increasing by the hour. Since the sighting in Devon, they had lost track of Elizabeth and Charles and although there were police in every town looking for them, there had been no further sightings.

Bertram was also on edge; he had sent Scotland Yard the note and the key to the storage locker in Briarwood and hadn't heard anything back from them. The detectives believed it was just one of Elizabeth's diversional tactics; but he wasn't so sure. If she had wanted him to divert his attention to Briarwood, she could have left the key at his home, instead of coming to Devon personally. Since this was the town where she had begun her murderous rampage, he knew that the storage locker must contain something she specifically wanted him to see.

With little to occupy his mind in Devon, Bertram began to prepare for his next seminar. He had already lost several days of work at the university and he didn't want to lose any more money. Although he and his wife lived a comfortable life in London, he couldn't afford to go without a pay packet for more than a few weeks. They had been planning for a family and he had already begun to build an extension on his home. This alone would cost nearly a year's wages.

A week, then two went by before Bertram heard what the officers had found in the storage locker. The news would be devastating. Inside the locker was a heavy trunk with no markings on the outside, but the police instantly realised it contained a body, as the smell of decay overwhelmed their senses.

The trunk was transferred in its entirety to the medical examiner. On opening it, the remains of an adult male were revealed. This elderly man was naked, but wrapped in newspaper clippings from all over London and several of these articles were from Manchester, relating to the murders of two men and a woman. The clipping that wrapped around the deceased's face was about a press conference held shortly after the bodies of these three victims had been found. The front page had a large picture of Richard Crombie and Detective Inspector Myers.

The medical examiner determined that the man inside the trunk had been dead for up to two months and had died from asphyxiation brought on by choking on his own vomit. It was not possible to determine whether poison was the culprit, but this was assumed.

The deceased would later be identified as Richard Crombie, former detective.

A letter glued to the inside lid of the trunk was addressed to Bertram. It read:

Dear Doctor Killam,

How does it feel to know that I have outsmarted you again? In fact, I have outsmarted everyone. Funny how you and everyone else thought my fate was already written. If only you had listened to me when I said I will never hang for my crimes. Maybe now you will see that I – and not you, nor anyone else – have control over my future and always will.

Poor, dear Richard, I must say he did put up a struggle, but in end, like always, I prevailed. Give my regards to your wife, Anna, she is a very lucky woman.

The medical examiner also determined that the note left inside the trunk had been put there recently. It was in pristine condition and had not yellowed or curled from the damp. The police knew that Elizabeth had also made a trip to Briarwood before going to Devon, yet no one had reported seeing her or Charles in the area.

Back in London, the police turned to their suspect's finances and were now trying to determine where Elizabeth had been keeping her money. She had several hundred pounds in her handbag when she was arrested, but since this was still in a locked safe, she had no access to it. The police knew that Elizabeth had continually bragged to her lawyer as well as the psychiatrists that she had enough money to live out her days in comfort, but no one could find any trace of it. The only other connection to the outside world she had, besides Charles, was her friend, Cathy Peirce, who was then brought in for questioning.

At first the detective treated Cathy as a witness, but she quickly became a person of interest when she told him that she was carrying Charles' baby. This connection could not be overlooked and as Detective Inspector Black questioned her further, an officer was on his way to search her home.

Cathy swore to Detective Inspector Black that she knew

nothing about Elizabeth's intentions, but when the officer said, 'How can you protect that monster? Do you know that she is responsible for disfiguring and murdering a fellow police officer's wife?'

Cathy replied in a whisper, 'You know Elizabeth one way, I know her in another and she does have another side to her that you have yet to see.' This enraged Detective Inspector Black who immediately had her thrown into a holding cell as he composed himself.

A thorough search of Cathy Peirce's large home did not reveal anything unusual. Like Elizabeth, Cathy had come into a great deal of money after her grandparents died and although the home was filled with antique furniture and paintings, it seemed empty of any evidence that would help solve this case.

There was also no one else living there, as Cathy's mother, Isabella Peirce, was living in France and her father had remarried and was no longer a part of her life.

Cathy was living off her inheritance in the same home where she had been raised after moving to London from her native Ireland. The detective established that she had not withdrawn a substantial amount of money recently so there was little evidence at this time to connect her to Elizabeth's escape. Still, there was something strange about the relationship she had with Elizabeth and Charles, so the detective decided to call Doctor Killam and ask that he return to London for a few days. The detective wanted him to assess her mental health and find out if she knew the difference between right and wrong. He also wanted to know if she knew where their suspects were hiding out and where Elizabeth was concealing her money.

At first Bertram refused, citing the safety of his wife and her family, but once he was assured that a police constable would keep an eye on them during his absence, he reluctantly agreed to go back to London. Like Detective Inspector Black, he did feel that Cathy's relationship with this couple was highly unusual, but at the time that he had spoken to her, he didn't feel that she was involved in any of the murders.

Arriving home after dark and feeling anxious about what Elizabeth would do next, he poured himself a large whisky, before retiring for the evening. The next morning, he awoke to the sound of something hitting the outside wall below his bedroom window. Upon further investigation, it appeared as though the men hired to do the extension had neglected to close the latch on the back door. Now as he prepared for his first session with Cathy Peirce, he hoped to wrap this up quickly so that he wouldn't be away from his wife any longer than he had to.

His first session with Cathy would begin on 28 November, exactly three weeks from the day that Elizabeth was to face the judge. To make her as comfortable as possible, he asked that the detective allow her to return home, considering her delicate condition.

Their first session would reveal a young woman who was shockingly insecure. Cathy had been raised by a cold, aloof mother and an absent father. She, like Elizabeth and Charles was an only child and had grown up with few friends. She had met Elizabeth when she was sixteen after being introduced to her by Charles. Elizabeth was just twelve when the three of them became inseparable. From that day forward, Cathy relied on her two friends for the attention she did not get at home. Elizabeth, it seemed, had begun manipulating her when she was just a young girl and had continued to do this until her own grandmother died.

This is when Elizabeth suddenly disappeared and Bertram realised that it was at the same time that she went to Briarwood.

To keep the communication lines open, Bertram concluded his first session with Cathy after less than two hours. However, the following day when he returned, Cathy's whole demeanour had changed. She had turned from a quiet, demure young woman, into a strangely aggressive one.

On the morning of the second day she greeted him wearing only her nightdress. Feeling somewhat embarrassed, he politely asked her to put on something more appropriate, but instead of doing what he asked, she began to slip it off over her head, revealing her very large belly and swollen breasts.

Bertram was at a loss for words and immediately took off his jacket and covered her. This didn't stop Cathy who then sat down within inches of him and attempted to give him a kiss.

It was now clear to Bertram that this young lady wasn't as stable as he had once believed. Unable to get through to her that morning, Bertram left shortly after he arrived. To avoid having this happen again, he asked Detective Inspector Black to move her sessions back into the interview room at the station. This, he believed, would make the sessions seem more formal and he hoped that he wouldn't have a repeat of her rather strange behaviour.

It had now been a month since Elizabeth escaped custody and no arrests had been made. Although the police had not determined how the two were funding their travels, Bertram would soon learn that Charles had been the one taking care of Elizabeth's money during her incarceration.

During the next session with Cathy, she had returned to normal and did not remember revealing her body to Bertram. In fact, she could barely remember the last time they had been together. This forgetfulness and strange behaviour wasn't common for someone of Cathy's age, but it did remind him of a seminar he had attended about people with split personality disorders and at that time, he had never come across one.

As he spoke to Cathy, he wondered if she was putting on an act or if she actually had two completely different personalities.

Today, she was shy and reserved and after Bertram explained what she had done the previous day, she wouldn't even make eye contact with him. This was an indicator that Cathy was not faking this sudden change and in retrospect, she did seem like a completely different person from the one he had met the day before.

As they talked that afternoon, she explained how Elizabeth took over where her mother left off. When Bertram asked her to elaborate, Cathy smiled as she explained how generous her friend could be. 'Elizabeth had the most exquisite taste in clothes and sometimes she would take me into the city and we would spend the entire day shopping, then she would treat me to a lovely dinner at the Plaza Hotel and we would sit and talk about our future plans.'

Bertram then asked, 'Was this the time that your mother had left home and made a new life in France?'

Cathy's expression changed to sadness, as she struggled to remember a painful time in her life. She diverted her eyes towards the window and tried to change the subject by commenting about the weather. 'Doesn't this awful rain get you down, doctor?'

Bertram smiled and replied, 'Yes, at times it does, but I suppose I am used to it now.' Bertram then reminded her of his question.

After a long pause she replied, 'My mother left for France right after Mr Riley was put to rest, leaving me alone with my ailing grandparents.'

Bertram then asked, 'Weren't you just a girl of sixteen at the time?'

Cathy looked directly in his eyes and replied, 'Yes, and you know, doctor, when I asked her if I could stay with her for a while, she said it was my duty to look after my grandparents and it was best that I remained in London for the foreseeable future!'

Bertram could see that this was upsetting for Cathy but she continued, 'You know, I never understood why she left when she did and all my mother would tell me was that Doctor Andrew Riley's death had affected her more than anyone will ever know.'

This made Bertram curious as to why Isabella Peirce would have reacted this way. Was it possible that she had been Andrew Riley's mistress? Richard Crombie had mentioned that Andrew had had some indiscretions, he never elaborated as to who they might have been with. Although he wanted to ask Cathy again about the possibility that she was related to Elizabeth, he decided by her sad expression that it was best not to proceed with this line of questioning.

Cathy's facial expressions changed again and she began to fidget and twirl her hair around her fingers nervously. This question seemed to bring back memories again that she found difficult to talk about. Still, Bertram was curious and he knew that Charles had introduced her to Elizabeth, just a few months before Mr and Mrs Riley were murdered. He wanted to know if she knew what her friend was about to do.

Bertram then asked if Elizabeth had ever talked openly about her mother and father.

Bertram also wanted to know how she had felt when Elizabeth, who was now implicated in her parents' murder, was taken to the psychiatric hospital where she could only visit her on occasion. Considering their relationship at the time, he wondered if this had an impact on her emotional well-being.

Cathy seemed to be struggling with his question and as she got up and looked out the window, Bertram remained seated and in a quiet, reassuring tone, he said, 'I know you and Elizabeth were very close when her parents died and I am sure you knew that she had taken their lives. Can you tell me how you felt when you heard what she had done? Did it have an impact on your friendship?'

Cathy returned to her chair and although she was no longer making eye contact with Bertram, she began to explain how she felt. 'We had been getting on so well until one afternoon when she saw Charles and me kissing. This is one of the only times she was ever angry with me and because I still wasn't aware of their relationship, I didn't understand why. I had come by to see her that day but her mother had caught her stealing money from her handbag, and she wasn't allowed visitors. When I got back to my house, Charles was there and one thing led to another. A few minutes later I heard Elizabeth scream, 'Get away from her, you bastard' and then suddenly she disappeared. This is when Charles finally told me about their relationship and, of course, at first I was shocked, I mean, she was just twelve years old.'

Although Cathy hadn't answered his question, Bertram didn't want to interrupt her, and she continued. 'You see, at the time, I accepted Charles for the way he was, but I didn't understand why he was attracted to a child. Still, I loved them both and I couldn't allow him to come between my friendship with Elizabeth, so instead of ending my relationship with him, I carried on with it and we both did everything we could to keep our affair secret.'

Cathy stopped talking suddenly, as if she had forgotten the original question and then asked if she could go home. Bertram could see her struggling to remember the question and replied, 'We have almost finished for today but can you just remind me about how you felt the day Elizabeth was taken out of her home by the police? Was it hard for you to accept the fact that she had murdered her parents?'

Cathy looked away before replying, 'Oh yes, I knew there was something you wanted to know. Shortly after the day she had seen Charles and me kissing, she came over to my house to bring me a gift. I can't remember what it was, but I do recall the beautiful paper it was wrapped in and the huge red bow that sat on top of the box. I think it was two days before Christmas: I remember feeling bad because I hadn't bought her anything. My grandmother was a very generous woman and when I told her what Elizabeth had done, she purchased a lovely silk scarf and insisted that Elizabeth have it. I think it was mid-afternoon on Christmas day when I brought it over to her house and saw that the police were there. I was worried that something had happened to her but they wouldn't allow me to go inside. The next day, Charles came by to tell me what had happened.'

Cathy became quiet again, leaving Bertram no other choice but to interrupt the silence by asking, 'Tell me, Cathy, was Charles involved in Mr and Mrs Riley's murder?' This question wasn't received very well, as out of nowhere Cathy's whole demeanour changed again, when she replied angrily, 'What murder? The Riley's weren't murdered! They died from food poisoning. Don't you remember? It was in all the papers?'

Bertram was fascinated by Cathy's loyalty and he knew she would only become defensive if he pressed her on this subject, so he asked, 'How did you feel when Elizabeth was taken to the psychiatric hospital?'

Cathy didn't respond right away and he could see she was still aggravated with him, but for some reason, a few minutes later, she looked up at him tearfully and replied, 'It was such a terrible time for all of us: Charles wasn't allowed to visit, but thankfully Mrs Crawford allowed me to go with her from time to time. Poor Elizabeth, we were all she had in the world and each time we went, she begged her grandmother to get her out of there. Mrs Crawford had been trying to do this for some time and finally, after almost four years, she was back home where she belonged. I remember how excited I was when I heard that she was getting out, but soon after this, her relationship with her grandmother became strained.'

At this time, Detective Inspector Black interrupted their conversation, pulled Bertram aside and insisted he hurry the session along. He just wanted to know if she was of sound mind and what, if anything, she could offer that would help them apprehend Elizabeth and Charles.

Bertram could see that the detective was finding his methods far too slow so he then moved along to the time that Elizabeth's grandmother had died and asked what Cathy remembered about this day.

Although Cathy was showing signs of increased anxiety, she did respond to his question. 'My mother was still in France and my grandmother was ill, so Elizabeth invited me to stay at her grandmother's, but this didn't turn out so well, because all they did was argue.'

When Bertram asked if she could recall what they argued about, she said, 'Oh yes, perfectly, you see, Marian was a lovely woman but sometimes Elizabeth tried to control her and she didn't like this.'

When asked to elaborate, Cathy said, 'One night when I was there, Elizabeth snuck downstairs and took out her granny's will and forged her name after she made some changes. Unfortunately, neither of us noticed that her grandmother was standing on the staircase. Elizabeth got caught doing the forgery. Right after, the two of them got into a horrible fight. Elizabeth got so angry that night that she even threatened to push her granny down the stairs. You see, doctor, Mrs Crawford's mind was as sharp as can be, but her body was failing and this is when Elizabeth's control over her became much, much, worse.'

When asked if she thought Elizabeth might have murdered her, she said, 'Oh yes, Elizabeth admitted this to Charles a few days after Mrs Crawford died. You see, when I told him what she had told me about her granny dying from heart failure, Charles laughed, and said that I was being naïve.' After a brief pause she added, 'Still, I wanted to believe that Elizabeth wouldn't have done such a thing because as you know, if not for her grandmother, she would have stayed where she was.'

Cathy seemed to recall everything so clearly, yet when Bertram tried to get her to repeat what she had said about Mrs Crawford's death to Detective Inspector Black, she looked at him as if she didn't remember that part of the conversation and said, 'What are you talking about?'

Bertram then asked the detective to leave and changed the subject by asking Cathy again why she didn't go to the police. This time her whole demeanour changed again and she raised her voice and said, 'Look, Bertram, I don't have to be here, I am not only doing you a great service, I am putting myself at risk, so do me a favour and stop asking the same damn questions!'

This personality change was much like how she had been when Bertram went to see her at her home and he wasn't certain how she had gone from a meek and mild young lady to one that sounded somewhat hysterical in such a short time.

Bertram found this new psychiatric phenomenon fascinating, but he knew the detective didn't. Detective Inspector Black wasn't the least bit interested in Cathy's apparent personality disorder and demanded that Bertram start to ask her direct questions, reminding him of the urgency. He wanted to know three things: first, was she still in contact with either of their suspects; second, did she know where Elizabeth or Charles had hidden their money; and last, did she have any idea where they might have gone.

Although Bertram explained that he couldn't rush her, in case she decided to keep these things to herself, the detective wouldn't listen. He wanted these answers and he wanted them now. Elizabeth and Charles were still on the run and the longer it took to capture these killers, the less likely it would be that they would be found. It had been over a month since Elizabeth escaped and they all feared that although the ports and railway stations were being guarded by police, it was possible that they had already left the country.

Cathy would remain combative throughout the rest of their session and she didn't seem to appreciate being interrupted several times by the same man that had treated her so rudely when she had first met him. Now she was refusing to answer any further questions about Elizabeth and Charles, so Bertram had no choice but to bring this session to a halt. Unfortunately, with Detective Inspector Black pressuring him for answers, his decision to stop for the day didn't go over very well.

Bertram realised he didn't have the proper training or knowledge to handle Cathy, but he knew who did.

That night, after having a very restless sleep, Bertram decided to bring in someone that was more familiar with people like Cathy and he called on an old colleague. Doctor Douglas Laird was now retired but he still did the odd seminar, when given a chance. At sixty-three he had been forced to retire and he was finding this new way of life to be quite boring. This being said, he was very excited to hear that Bertram had come across a woman that may have two very different personalities. He referred to a case in Germany where another woman had been diagnosed in 1905 as having 'dissociative disorder'. She had three personalities, all of which were completely different from one another. Doctor Laird happily agreed to meet with Bertram the following day to observe Cathy Peirce and possibly offer some advice.

Bertram explained that there was some urgency in finding the answers for Detective Inspector Black and even if he did believe that she had this disorder, he would still have to ask her these questions. This was completely understandable and Doctor Laird said he might be able to help ascertain the answers to these questions, once he met her face to face.

Finding Elizabeth

The next morning, Cathy Peirce was brought in to the station kicking and screaming. According to the police, Cathy initially refused to come with them and slammed the door in their face. A call was then made to Detective Inspector Black, who insisted she be brought in, despite her refusals and this seemed to have led to the crucial witness's outlandish response.

That same day, Detective Inspector Black held a news conference to update the public about Elizabeth Riley and Charles Rigley. In it, he did something that Bertram and later, Doctor Laird would refer to as incompetent. He announced that they had a witness that was helping the investigation and then named Cathy Peirce. This was not wise for obvious reasons, and now with the newspapers about to run with this story, he had just put Miss Peirce's life at unnecessary risk.

The detective would end the news conference that morning, by offering an unprecedented £500.00 reward, for any information that would lead to their arrest.

17

Just before their session began, Bertram pulled Doctor Laird aside and told him that he had seen Cathy Peirce acting quite bizarre, but never like this. The first time he met Cathy, she was shy and quiet; now she was exhibiting further signs of hysteria. Doctor Laird was fascinated, commenting, 'This could possibly mean that she has three personalities, just like the young girl in Germany.'

It would take almost an hour to calm Cathy down that morning and when she was finally soothed, she tucked her head into her knees and began rocking back and forth.

Bertram spoke softly as he asked her the first question that the detective wanted to know: 'Can you think of anywhere that Charles or Elizabeth might be hiding their money?'

Cathy's whole demeanour suddenly changed. She diverted her eyes from Bertram and then replied, 'Of course I do, Charles kept a safe at my home that contained every penny of Elizabeth's inheritance and I believe there had to be at least £7,000 in there.'

When asked if it was still there, she said, 'Oh heavens no, he removed it a few months before Elizabeth was arrested at the café.'

He then asked her to recall exactly when this occurred and she swore she couldn't remember, then a few seconds later she replied, 'Oh dear, was it a few months ago, or was it last week, I'm so sorry, my memory has been causing me problems since I was a child.'

Doctor Laird noticed several telltale signs that made him believe that Cathy did in fact have the condition he had described to Bertram. Dissociative disorder patients often struggle with their memories and they are also extremely forgetful as their dominant personality will tend to jumble their thoughts.

A few minutes later, Bertram unknowingly set Cathy back into a rage, when he asked, 'Do you have any idea where Charles and Elizabeth might be going now?'

For some reason, this question upset her and suddenly she stood up, walked directly towards Bertram, leaned over him and shouted, 'What on earth are you talking about? Charles loves me and he has not gone anywhere with that whore!'

Bertram was quite surprised at her response; this was the first time he had seen any outward animosity from Cathy towards Elizabeth.

As Cathy sat with her arms folded staring at the floor, Doctor Laird then turned to Bertram and asked, 'Shall I give this a try?'

Bertram replied, 'Please do.'

As Bertram slowly backed away from Cathy, Doctor Laird asked her in a low, calming voice, 'Miss Peirce, I understand completely that you are upset, but I also understand why the police need to find Elizabeth Riley. Now if you bear with us for just a little while longer, I promise this line of questioning will end very soon.'

Cathy sat back down, but he could see that it would take a little longer to bring her back to the woman they had been just talking to before her outburst.

Doctor Laird turned to Bertram and said, 'I bet this lovely young woman would like a cup of tea and maybe she would enjoy a couple of biscuits too.'

Cathy smiled at Doctor Laird and said in a quiet, barely audible voice, 'Oh, yes, that would be lovely.'

Bertram took his cue and left to find the kettle. It was obvious to him that Doctor Laird had some experience with this disorder and if anyone could get through to Cathy, it was him.

Bertram then took his time as he made some tea and gathered a few biscuits from the station's makeshift kitchen. It was best to leave her in the hands of a doctor that had experience with this and he knew that the longer he stayed away, the more likely it was that she would open up to Doctor Laird.

Ten minutes later he returned with the tea and as he opened the door, he could hear Cathy laughing. She had taken to Doctor Laird and he had told her a story that she seemed to enjoy. As Bertram placed the tea beside her, she looked up, smiled, and then thanked him.

Doctor Laird glanced over at him and Bertram could tell that it was best that he remained quiet. He then sat back, lit a cigarette and began taking notes. Learning something new from this brilliant doctor was an honour and he could immediately see Cathy was not only answering his questions, she was interacting with him, just like she had done on the first day that he had met her.

Once they had finished their tea, Doctor Laird asked her if it would be all right to talk about Elizabeth and Charles again. Cathy smiled at the doctor, replying, 'Of course.'

Doctor Laird then tapped her hand in a reassuring manner, saying, 'I understand that Charles took his safe the last time he was at your home, now tell me do you recall when that was?'

Cathy looked as if she was trying to remember something, then she went into her handbag and pulled out her diary. As she turned the pages she looked confused. Finally, she turned to a page and stopped, saying, 'Did I tell you I have problems remembering things?'

Doctor Laird winked at Bertram and replied, 'No, I don't think you did, but you know, dear, I have that same problem too.'

'Then,' Cathy said, looking directly at Doctor Laird, 'you must carry a diary. It's the best way to keep track of things.'

The doctor gently patted her hand again and thanked her for the advice. 'So, does that little book tell you when Charles collected his safe?'

Cathy looked down at the page she had stopped at and said, 'November the first, that's when he came by. It was so wonderful to see him and he seemed so happy to hear that I was with child. You know, Doctor Laird, I think Charles will be a wonderful father, don't you?'

This seemed to go along with the timeline. If Charles and Elizabeth had discussed her escape during the time he had worked as her guard, then of course she would have told him to get her money.

Doctor Laird could see that Cathy loved Charles and replied, 'Yes, I'm sure he would be a wonderful father.' It was obvious that this was the answer she wanted to hear.

Cathy turned to Bertram. 'I think you were asking about where Charles might have gone, so it's a good thing I wrote down the town.'

Bertram didn't press her, waiting while she looked through her diary again.

A few seconds later she said, 'Oh here it is, he's gone to Somerset on business.' She added, 'That's funny, he said he would only be gone for a week or so and I think he should be back by now.'

Cathy was starting to fidget, so Doctor Laird suggested Bertram arrange for a constable to take her home.

Doctor Laird was wise and as Bertram walked Cathy out to the waiting carriage, she abruptly turned to him and said loudly, 'What do you want now? Haven't you bothered me enough in recent days?' Again, Cathy was acting as though she had forgotten their session that had only occurred five minutes ago.

Although Bertram wasn't accustomed to this rare psychosis, Doctor Laird assured him that it was quite common in patients with dissociative disorder and this is why he had decided to end the session when he did.

Bertram told Detective Inspector Black what Cathy had revealed then spoke with Doctor Laird. To his pleasure, as it had been a trying day, Laird suggested they go for a quiet drink.

Over the next hour or so the two doctors discussed Cathy Peirce and why Elizabeth might have spared her life. They concluded that her poor mental health had probably been the reason and it was also the same reason why Elizabeth had developed a relationship with her in the first place.

As Doctor Laird had said that afternoon, 'People are often drawn to similar people, you know, my boy. It's human nature and although these women have very different psychological impairments, it is obvious that Cathy needed direction when she met Elizabeth and at the same time, Elizabeth needed a friend.'

Bertram hadn't thought about it this way. He had delved into the life of Elizabeth Riley and all he could see within her was her psychosis. He really didn't think about her need to have a friend, or for that matter her need to interact with other girls of a similar age. Elizabeth may have only been twelve when she first met Cathy, but her intelligence and mannerisms were of someone much older. Cathy was almost four years Elizabeth's senior but she was far more innocent than Elizabeth had ever been.

Cathy's grandparents were probably aware that Cathy was different and so they had sheltered her from real life. She may have appeared fully developed physically but she had the emotional stability of a girl much younger. This also made it easy for Charles to manipulate her. Working in the background, the detectives of Scotland Yard had discovered that he was highly educated, extremely charming and had a long history of associations with girls much younger them himself.

Bertram realised that Doctor Laird, who was not only his mentor but an old friend, could still teach him much more about the human psyche than he could learn in a lifetime. Now he regretted not attending more of the older man's seminars when he had the chance to do so. His skill in persuading people with psychological disorders to open up to him was unmatched by any other medic Bertram knew. He hoped that some day, he could take what he learned from Doctor Laird and make a positive difference in someone else's life.

As the two said their goodbyes, Doctor Laird reassured Bertram that he would keep an eye on Cathy, and possibly, if she allowed, he would visit her at home to see how she was getting on.

Bertram had done what he had come to London to do and now he hoped that Cathy's information would be just what the police would need to capture Elizabeth and Charles. His only concern was Cathy's well-being. He hoped that even if Elizabeth had learned about her pregnancy, she would leave her be.

Bertram would leave London the following day full of hope for a future that was free from Elizabeth Riley. To make his journey a little less boring, he had gathered up a few textbooks from his university days to read on his long train ride back to Devon. Cathy Peirce had sparked Bertram's interest in dissociative disorders and during his next seminar, he planned on introducing this rather rare phenomenon to his audience.

As he sat in the train preparing to leave London for the foreseeable future, he thought about Richard Crombie and how this man in such a brief time had made such a huge impact on the way he thought about police and their techniques.

Bertram had never been a fan of authority and although he followed the rules, he often thought of the police as cruel and uncaring when it came to those suffering from different forms of mental illness. Now as he sat watching London's smoky skyline disappear, he wondered when the coroner would release Crombie's remains for the interment, which he hoped he could attend.

Richard Crombie was Elizabeth's last known victim. All the other victims had been released for burial; but Richard's body was still being held in cold storage and this didn't seem fair, or necessary.

Bertram had been away from his wife for some days now and he was very anxious to see her and discuss the patient he had assessed, but the minute he saw her face at the railway station he knew that there was something very wrong.

During his absence Anna had received a disturbing letter from Elizabeth:

Dear Anna,
It was wonderful to take a walk down memory lane and look through your lovely wedding album. You were such a beautiful bride, and, of course, Bertram was a truly handsome groom.

How nice it was to see your home and despite its location and size, I see you have done your best with what you have. Charles and I found your bed to be extremely comfortable, but you might want to change those draughty windows. Funny how sleeping on a hard cot for weeks on end can make you appreciate even the most ordinary things in life. I just know that if the circumstances were different we could have been the best of friends, maybe someday we will.
E. Riley.

Bertram was mortified and now he realised that the uneasy feeling he had experienced when he arrived home in London wasn't his imagination. He now recalled how the back door had swung open and woke him up the next morning. He had originally put the blame on the neglectful workmen that were completing the extension and now he believed that this was how Elizabeth had entered his home.

This was most disturbing and the more he thought about this, the more concerned he became. Although he knew that this must have been weeks earlier, he decided to call Detective Inspector Black and let him know.

Anna was now talking about selling their home in London. She didn't feel that she would ever be safe again and the thought of Elizabeth being in her marital bed turned her stomach.

'I understand your concern,' Bertram said. 'We cannot sell the house at this time. But I will purchase a new bed immediately.'

This wasn't enough for Anna and for the next few days she refused to talk to him. It wasn't until Bertram realised how truly frightened his wife had been after receiving this letter that he finally gave in and agreed to sell the house.

Anna meant the world to him and he wasn't going to allow a psychopath to come between them. Elizabeth's need to be in control had now spilled into his wife's life and caused her extreme anxiety, but there wasn't much he could do about this, except support his wife and sell the home that he had worked so hard to achieve. To reassure her he wrote to his bank manager and asked him to begin the process.

Back in Briarwood, Detective Inspector Cross received word that Richard Crombie's body was ready to be released for burial. Knowing that Bertram would want to attend the funeral, he called his home but didn't receive an answer, as Bertram was still in Devon.

Of course, Bertram did not see the announcement about Richard Crombie's funeral in the local papers in Yorkshire. As a result he missed paying his last respects to a man he truly admired. On 11 December, with more than 200 officers from all over England attending, Richard Crombie was laid to rest beside his beloved wife.

Bertram heard about the funeral on 20 December when he received a newspaper clipping in the post. The clipping had a photo of the cemetery and showed the massive police presence, as well as some of the mourners standing around the detective's grave. As he looked closer, he noticed that someone had drawn a circle around a woman's head. She was wearing a black frock and had a veil over her face to conceal her appearance. The very next day Bertram received a letter from Elizabeth to confirm it was her.

My dearest Bertram,
I wanted to write to let you know how much I enjoyed Richard Crombie's funeral. For a man with few friends, he certainly drew a crowd. My only complaint has to be the food served afterwards. Dear

God, I don't understand how some people can eat such garbage, but don't you worry, Bertram, when you die, I will certainly make sure you have a proper send-off and a delightful meal afterwards. Always and forever, Elizabeth.

18

Thankfully, Anna had not seen that letter and Bertram had no intentions of showing it to her. He did, however, send telegrams to Detective Inspector Black in London and Detective Inspector Cross in Yorkshire to let them know that Elizabeth had been in Briarwood again.

Cross thanked him for the information, but Black responded curtly that he would gladly put the noose around Elizabeth's neck when she was found. This cat-and-mouse game was obviously getting on the detective's nerves.

Bertram could certainly understand the London detective's frustration, but when he requested an officer to watch his home, he was flatly turned down. Detective Inspector Black, unapologetic, and filled with anger, responded by return telegram with a flat *not possible*.

It was very apparent that the police were overwhelmed. Bertram and his family were on their own and shouldn't expect any help unless Elizabeth actually showed up. Now it was up to Bertram to decide what to do next. Elizabeth's letter held underlying threats, but he wasn't concerned about his own safety. His wife and her elderly parents were his priority and he would do whatever it took to keep them safe. Mr and Mrs Coburn had lived in this home for over forty years and the thought of asking them to move weighed heavy on his shoulders. Bertram certainly didn't want to reveal Elizabeth's letter, but he knew that if he had to, he would, if only to encourage them that her threats should be taken very seriously.

As he lay in bed with his wife that night, he stared up at the ceiling trying to find the right words to tell her that her family may have to leave their matrimonial home, at least until Elizabeth and Charles were apprehended. Elizabeth had turned his world upside down and now he felt like he was going to do the same to his wife and her family. As he recalled the day he met Elizabeth, nothing about this would have warned him what was coming. He assumed – like everyone else – that she would be tried, convicted and hanged for her crimes.

It wasn't until the very last few days of their time together that he had begun to feel very uneasy about some of the things she was saying. Still, how could he have predicted any of this? Keeping her under lock and key had been the responsibility of the police and the prison service. And in hindsight the police should have looked into her accomplice. But they did not think to find him after she was arrested.

As Anna slept soundly beside him, Bertram knew he would have to come clean and tell her and her parents about this new letter. Although he worried about their reactions, he knew that not being honest with them could put them all in grave danger.

With Christmas less than three days away, he decided to keep this to himself for a little while longer. Bertram's priority was his family, but this time of the year was always very special for his wife as 25 December was also the day she was born.

As the family gathered around the dining room table on Christmas night, Bertram was asked to say a prayer. As he thanked God for his family, his health and the abundance that he was about to partake in, he opened his eyes briefly to see that his wife had tears running down her face.

Anna had a secret too, one which she didn't want to share with anyone. She had felt her baby stirring inside her but during the last few days it hadn't moved. Bertram didn't even know she was with child and when she finally told him that night, he immediately went for the local doctor. He couldn't do much to ease her mind about Elizabeth Riley, but he could at least find out if her fear was real or imagined.

Doctor Carter had been the family physician for over thirty years. He had also delivered Anna twenty-two years earlier. He was out on a call when Bertram went to his home, but his wife promised that he would come by the following morning to check for a foetal heartbeat. 'Don't worry, Doctor Killam,' she said. 'It's not unusual to feel very little movement early on, especially if it's her first.' These reassuring words didn't convince Anna that her child was still alive and the next morning she was so anxious that she refused to get out of bed.

Doctor Carter was good for his word and at 9am he came by to see a very distraught young woman. As Bertram sat by Anna's side, holding her hand, Doctor Carter put his stethoscope on her belly and after what seemed like an eternity, he announced loudly that the foetus was alive and well.

Anna was so relieved she immediately jumped out of bed and hugged him tightly. Bertram then walked the doctor to his carriage and they talked about the stress everyone in the household was under.

Doctor Carter looked grave. 'You know that worry can cause a miscarriage. Keep her free from stress as far as possible.'

With these words ringing in his ears, even before the sound of Doctor Carter's carriage wheels had died away, Bertram took the letter and newspaper article that Elizabeth had sent to him out of his side table and threw it into the fire. To show this to Anna now would only increase her anxiety.

～

Back in London, Cathy Peirce was now being followed day and night as reporters were hounding her for a story. Doctor Laird had met with her after Bertram left and told her that she should not talk to the reporters. He also warned her to avoid having her picture taken.

Cathy, who had believed that she was about five months pregnant, was in fact, closer to seven. Her belly was unmistakable now and by the way her mind was confusing her, the doctor felt that she certainly wasn't prepared for this child. But she trusted Doctor Laird and continued to allow him to check on her from time to time.

He also arranged for her to be seen by a very knowledgeable midwife who would be visiting her regularly. Although the midwife found Cathy to be somewhat difficult at times she had known Doctor Laird for a number of years and would not let him down.

～

By mid-January of 1914, Bertram had not yet gone back to London to sign the necessary papers and arrange for the sale of his home. He did not want to leave his wife in her condition and he wanted to be there to intercept any post from Elizabeth that may arrive at her family's home.

Anna no longer pressured Bertram to move forward with the house sale and she definitely felt much safer when he was there with her. With no sightings of Elizabeth and Charles in Devon since the farmer had seen them, and no further deaths that could be linked to them, the urgency to make an arrest was beginning to subside.

The nation's police had turned their attention to a sequential killer in Liverpool who had taken the lives of four prostitutes.

As Elizabeth's case went cold, Bertram was trying to figure out where his next pay packet would come from. His absence from the university didn't go unnoticed and after missing an entire month of work, he received a letter of dismissal. Bertram also missed his last seminar and although he was given the option of another date in early February, he decided it was in his wife's best interest that he stay in Devon, at least until his baby was delivered. Doctor Carter expected Anna to give birth in early June and for now Bertram would use his savings to continue his payments on the house he owned in London.

In the meantime, Cathy was doing her best to stay away from the reporters but on 22 January, a reporter convinced her to have a series of pictures taken. He had lied and said he would not use these photos until she gave permission to do so.

Bertram had no idea that this had happened until the afternoon of 16 February when he received another letter from Elizabeth. Inside the envelope were several front-page photos of Cathy Peirce and a series of articles that clearly stated who the child's father was. The headline of one read, *How will Elizabeth Riley react when Cathy Peirce delivers her lover's baby?* Charles was named throughout these articles and Bertram knew that Charles and Cathy could be in danger of retaliation.

A letter addressed to Bertram inside the envelope read:

My darling Bertram,
I understand that we will both become parents very soon and although I won't be going through that dreadful pain during delivery, I will certainly become a mother.

All I can hope for is that this child takes after his father, you know, he is such a handsome man and he does have the loveliest smile.
So, as we both prepare for our children, I do hope you are taking very good care of your dear, sweet wife. Give her my love.
Elizabeth.

Bertram began to panic. Detective Inspector Black had put Cathy in harm's way and now he could not turn his back on her.

Without telling Anna, Bertram went to the nearest post office and placed a call to Doctor Laird. He had already seen the article and was also very frightened for Cathy. 'I have told her to go either to her mother's home in France, or come here to stay with me until the birth. But alas, she refused.' All he could do now was keep a closer watch on her and pray that Elizabeth would leave her be.

Doctor Laird believed that Elizabeth might be just toying with him again, like she had during their sessions, but Bertram wasn't as confident and he now worried about Cathy Peirce's future. He also felt terribly guilty because it was he that had originally told Aubrie about her connection to Charles.

Once Bertram finished speaking to Doctor Laird, he immediately called Detective Inspector Black to voice his concerns. This time the London detective was more receptive, but all he could promise was that an officer would go by Cathy's home twice a day to check on her.

Over the next couple of weeks Cathy remained at home without incident. She now had police officers, her midwife and Doctor Laird checking up on her and everything seemed to be going as planned.

Cathy was happily awaiting the arrival of her child and she would deliver her healthy, seven-pound son on 3 March with few complications. To Doctor Laird's surprise she had not experienced any further dissociative episodes since his birth. At this time, he couldn't say if they would return, but he did think that this was a good sign and that this may be some sort of remission.

Cathy would remain under the watchful eye of the police for several weeks after giving birth, but a little less than two months later, the Metropolitan Police Commissioner suddenly ordered that the patrols past her house be stopped. Bertram was not notified. Still, as far as he knew, she was safe and had not heard from either Elizabeth or Charles since the baby's birth.

As spring arrived without any further communication from Elizabeth, Bertram began to concentrate his efforts on finding another home he could bring his growing family to. He only had a few weeks left before his wife was to give birth and her parent's home was already feeling crowded.

Anna and Bertram had begun to talk about leaving London entirely, but he knew that he would eventually have to go back to work. With her heart being set on never returning, he decided to apply for work to universities in other parts of the country.

Bertram was a highly respected criminal psychiatrist and it didn't take long before the University of Wales responded. They were offering a two-year contract, starting at a salary just below what he had been earning in London. Considering the cost of living was much lower in Wales than it was in London, this was a reasonable offer. When he told Anna about it, she was thrilled and insisted that he take the job starting in September of that same year. Anna had spent some of her summers in Wales when she was a child and she had fond memories of that time.

A few days later, after an excruciatingly long labour, Anna gave birth to a six-pound, seven-ounce baby girl, who they named Margaret Ann, after Bertram's late grandmother. Bringing a new life into this world give Bertram and his wife some hope that sooner or later, their lives would return to normal.

But his new-found happiness would be shattered when he received another letter from Elizabeth. In it she wrote:

My dearest Bertram,
I believe congratulations are in order. How lovely to hear that Anna has given you a daughter.
I will keep this letter relatively short as I have a few things to take care of after this and I promise you that there may only be one other, perhaps two more letters, before I disappear for a while.
You, my love, have received the most precious gift of all, a baby girl, who will always look up to you and make you feel like you are the most important person in her life.
Now, this being said, I would be rude if I didn't give you a gift too. All you have to do is go back to your home and find it. I promise that you won't be disappointed.
Now don't you worry, darling, I am nowhere near Devon at the moment, and your dear, sweet wife and child are perfectly safe.
Unlike some people who will remain nameless at this time, I can be relied upon.
Forever in my thoughts,
Elizabeth

19

The first thought that came to Bertram's mind was how on earth Elizabeth had known about his infant daughter when he had purposely refrained from putting out a notice.

The next thing that puzzled him was this gift she had mentioned. What could she have left in his home in London that he would be the least bit interested in? And how had she done it? Besides the police that regularly made their rounds nearby, he had at least three of his neighbours constantly checking to see if anything was amiss.

He was also worried that this was a ruse to get him there. He recalled the letter that mentioned his funeral and wondered, was she setting him up for an ambush? Knowing what Elizabeth was capable of, this only worried him more.

His mind was racing. In order to be rid of Elizabeth for good, he would have to sell their home and move away, but the only way to do this was to go back, sign the papers and prepare it for sale. Then again, what if Elizabeth was there? And if she wasn't, could he be sure that she would stay away from Anna and his newborn daughter? Thinking about this just caused his head to ache, but he knew he would have to do something and the sooner, the better.

At this time, neither Anna nor her parents knew that Elizabeth had continued to write to him. This made his life more difficult. Knowing he couldn't take Anna and the baby with him and that he wouldn't be here to protect them just made him more anxious.

As Bertram sat looking down at this beautiful little miracle that he and his wife had created, he suddenly remembered an old friend that owed him a favour. Jack Calhoun, a retired police officer, lived just a few miles down the road from Anna's parents.

Bertram had met Jack years ago when his wife had taken to her bed suffering from depression. Using his skills as a medic, he had gone out of his way to help Mrs Calhoun through this and in time, she recovered fully. Now Bertram needed his services and after another sleepless night, he went to see Jack before Anna was up that morning and ask him if he would consider staying at Mr and Mrs Coburn's home during his absence. Bertram knew this was a lot to ask of his friend, but at this time, his options were limited.

Although Jack had been retired for several years, he was aware of the role Bertram had played during Elizabeth Riley's incarceration. He was also aware of how dangerous she could be and when Bertram explained why he had to return to London for up to two weeks, he wholeheartedly agreed to stay with Bertram's family for as long as was needed. His wife, Gertrude was forever grateful for all of Bertram's help and although she had been gone for almost three years now, Jack had never forgotten what he had done for them.

On 18 June, after a tearful goodbye, Bertram reluctantly boarded the train, expecting to be gone for up to two weeks.

As the train departed that morning, he tried to use some of the techniques he had taught others to calm himself down.

Although Anna didn't know anything about Elizabeth's letters, she seemed very nervous about this trip he was taking. It was difficult to reassure her, when he couldn't reassure himself and he certainly didn't know what to expect when he got back to London.

His gut told him to prepare for the worst and although he would be exhausted from his trip, he wisely did this. Bertram decided it was best that he first go to Scotland Yard and request that a constable accompany him. But on this night, the Yard did better for him. Detective Inspector Black took one look at the letter Bertram had received from Elizabeth and he agreed to accompany him.

It was very late when they arrived, and Bertram's anxiety grew as they neared his home. He didn't have any idea what he was about to face that night but when he arrived, he was happy to see that his home was in total darkness.

Nothing from the street indicated that anyone was still inside as Bertram turned the key, but the moment they opened the door they were taken aback by the horrific smell. The detective immediately blew on his whistle to attract the attention of nearby beat constables. Bertram was beside himself with anger and he hit the door with his fist.

When the officers arrived, Bertram was sitting on his doorstep sobbing. His first thought went directly to Cathy Peirce. Someone was dead in his home and she was the likely victim. Detective Inspector Black tried to comfort him, but by now Bertram was so filled with anger that all he could say was, 'If she's dead, this, sir, is down to you!'

Bertram was told to wait outside as the officers entered his home, all holding their handkerchiefs over their mouths. Whoever was inside was decomposing rapidly. The smell would take weeks, possibly months to disappear from his home.

As Bertram smoked one cigarette after another, the officers

were going through his house that was now considered a crime scene. Fifteen minutes later, Detective Inspector Black came out and asked Bertram to follow him. After searching through all the rooms, the deceased was found in Bertram's bedroom and it wasn't Cathy Peirce.

The decomposing body of Charles Rigley was sitting in an oversized chair wearing Bertram's nightshirt. His mouth had been sewn shut and in his right hand, he held his own penis. His eyes were eerily fixed on a photo that sat on a side table. The photo was obviously altered by Elizabeth, as she had placed herself beside Bertram in his original wedding photo. Glued to his left hand was a bloodied photo of Cathy and her infant son.

The scene was so disturbing that two of the officers trembled as they gathered the evidence Elizabeth had left behind.

Bertram became inconsolable when he saw that Elizabeth had replaced each of their wedding photos with images of herself. And she had worn his wife's wedding dress, which he later found thrown on the bathroom floor, covered in her lover's blood.

At this time, the only victim found inside Bertram's home was Charles Rigley and although Bertram was relieved that it wasn't Cathy Peirce, he demanded that two officers immediately be dispatched to check on Cathy and her infant son.

An hour later, the officers returned to let Bertram know that the initial search of her home revealed nothing out of the ordinary. There was no evidence that Elizabeth had even been there, or had harmed her or her child and no one was inside the home when they arrived. It also appeared as though nothing outside her home had been disturbed.

Bertram's home would remain sealed for the next few days

as the investigation continued. The body of Charles Rigley was removed the next morning and taken to the coroner's office. It would be determined that he had died from exsanguination after his penis had been severed. He seemed to have been dosed with a unknown sedative; but the coroner believed he was at least partially aware of what was going on before succumbing to the blood loss.

Bertram never entered his home again after that dreadful night and he remained in London for just two more days before selling his home back to the bank for far less than he would have received on an open market.

Elizabeth contacted him one last time before Bertram finally took his wife, child and her parents out of Devon and moved to an undisclosed location.

In her letter dated 9 July but with no visible postmark, Elizabeth wrote:

My darling Bertram,
I do hope you enjoyed my little surprise. It was so much fun watching Charles gasp for air as he slowly bled to death.
I can only imagine the look on your face when you saw him, of course, slightly less masculine than he once was. Still, I have to admit that I had the greatest pleasure removing his organ. You do know that he deserved this, don't you, dear?
Anyhow, I just wanted to let you know that I feel so welcome in my new home that I will probably stick around for a while. I can only imagine the dreury weather in England right now, the dark skies and rainy days are enough to drive one crazy. Although it's a little colder here, the sunshine overhead is just enough to brighten my days.
Don't you worry, my love, I will try my best to behave myself but I can't promise that this will last. Like I was told time and again, I am a true psychopath with little hope for a normal life or for that matter, as I was also told, little hope to stay alive past my twenty-first birthday.

Can you imagine that some cheeky psychiatrist actually said that to me? Maybe he was right. What do you think, Bertram? Can I live a normal life or will I get bored one day and leave you to pick up the pieces. For now, I plan on settling into my new life. But if I were you, I wouldn't get too comfortable because I can assure you that this will not last forever. Now, don't forget to give my love to Anna and Margaret Ann.
Forever in my thoughts, Elizabeth.

THE END

ACKNOWLEDGEMENTS

I would like to acknowledge my husband Chris. He had always been supportive and he has spent countless hours listening to my stories as I read them out loud during my final edits.

I would also like to thank my beautiful daughter Kristin, who has helped me through some challenging times as well as being instrumental in helping me solve my various computer issues that seem to crop up from time to time.

My two closest friends, Kim and Sandy. They have both not only been with me through the good and bad times, they are currently my biggest fans!

Last but not least are my sibling. Robert who is also a published writer and my sister Susan. We may not see each other much during these trying times, but we will always remain very close...

Printed in Germany
by Amazon Distribution
GmbH, Leipzig